EX LIBRIS

Jacob Portman

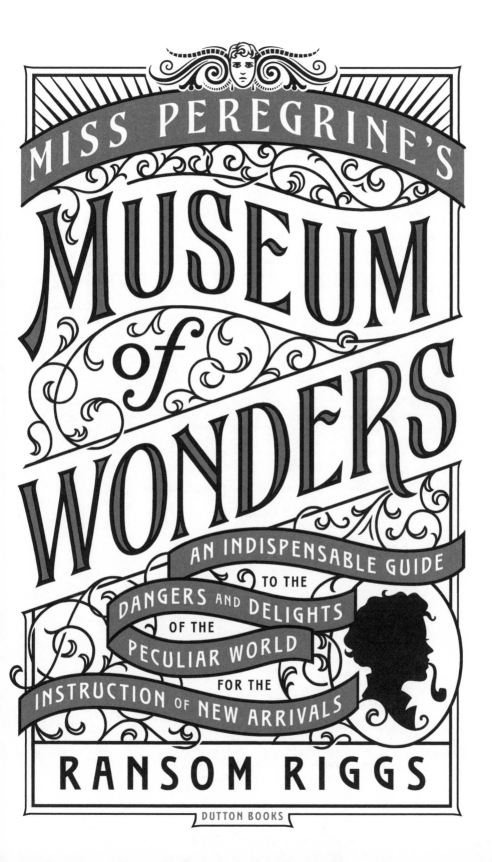

MISS PEREGRINE'S MUSEUM of WONDERS

AN INDISPENSABLE GUIDE TO THE DANGERS AND DELIGHTS OF THE PECULIAR WORLD FOR THE INSTRUCTION OF NEW ARRIVALS

RANSOM RIGGS

DUTTON BOOKS

DUTTON BOOKS

An imprint of Penguin Random House LLC, New York

First published in the United States of America by Dutton Books,
an imprint of Penguin Random House LLC, 2022

To peculiar children everywhere.
You are not alone.

To Jacob,
I hope you find this volume illuminating.
With great admiration,
Miss P

Miss Alma Le Fay Peregrine

Miss Peregrine's
MUSEUM *of* WONDERS

AN INDISPENSABLE GUIDE TO THE DANGERS AND DELIGHTS OF THE PECULIAR WORLD FOR THE INSTRUCTION OF NEW ARRIVALS

BY

Alma L. Peregrine, editor

AUTHOR OF SEVERAL FORMIDABLE WORKS:
How to Appear Normal
Certain Death and How to Avoid it
and *Fifty-Two Loops to See in a Lifetime*

CONTAINING

ESSENTIAL FACTS; ASTOUNDING TALES;
STRANGE EVENTS OF HISTORY; LIFE-PRESERVING
INSTRUCTIONS FOR TEMPORAL TRAVEL; ZOOLOGICAL
WONDERS; HISTORICAL BATTLES; UNFORTUNATE
OCCURRENCES; EMINENT INDIVIDUALS YOU MIGHT
NOT HAVE REALIZED WERE PECULIAR; EXCERPTS FROM
IMPORTANT PECULIAR MANUSCRIPTS; RUDE JOKES AND
HUMOROUS CONTRIVANCES; POSTHUMOUS OBSERVATIONS
BY UNDEAD ACQUAINTANCES; COLORFUL PHRASES IN
THE OLD PECULIAR LANGUAGE; CAPTIVATING INCIDENTS
AND PECULIAR ADVENTURES; AMUSING LISTS AND NON-
ESSENTIAL TRIVIA; ALLIES AND ENEMIES WHOM EVERY
PECULIAR SHOULD KNOW; QUACKS AND CHARLATANS;
TECHNIQUES FOR QUICK ESCAPE; A PECULIAR
"PENNY DREADFUL"

EXCESSIVELY ILLUSTRATED WITH
NUMEROUS CAPTIVATING PHOTOGRAVURES
A NON-TRIVIAL NUMBER OF WOODCUT ENGRAVINGS
SEVERAL ESSENTIAL MAPS NEVER BEFORE PRINTED
AND ONE SCRAWL DRAWN ON A NAPKIN BY A CHILD
WHICH NEARLY ENDED LIFE AS WE KNOW IT

ALSO INCLUDING INSTRUCTIONS ON HOW TO
LOCATE HIDDEN TIME LOOPS
TELL IF SOMEONE IS NORMAL OR FAKING IT
LIVE UNDETECTED AMONG NORMALS
ESCAPE A RAMPAGING HOLLOWGAST
FIND SECRET CHAMBERS AND HIDING PLACES
FAKE YOUR OWN DEATH
MAKE VARIOUS AND DIVERS WHIRLIGIGS
AND MUCH MORE.

A CAVEAT FOR THE UNWARY

This book is meant for peculiar eyes only. The publisher will not be held responsible for what might occur should unauthorized persons read it.

INTRODUCTION

You are being hunted.

Right now, at this very moment, there are unspeakable creatures whispering your name and lusting for your blood. If you weren't already aware of this, I'm sorry to be the one to tell you. I don't relish the task, but you must know what you're up against. There are other dangers, besides: sudden, rapid aging; faulty time loops; mercenary peculiars. Normals whose fear of the unknown—and you—can quickly turn to anger, and violence. If you're aware of your own peculiarness, be in no doubt: Others are, too. And be they normal, wightish, or hollowgast, they want nothing good for you. They want to exploit you, subjugate you, even steal your very soul.

There was a time when all we had to worry about was being burned at the stake. It was a simpler world then.

Not to say there aren't pleasures in being peculiar. On the

contrary, there are many. But since my sworn duty as an ymbryne is to keep you safe, I do tend to focus on the terrifying and terrible. So long as I've got your attention, there are other things you might like to know about who we are and how we live. To survive as a peculiar, you must understand our enemies. But to thrive, you must understand *us*, and our unique society.

I might have called this book *So You're a Peculiar, Now What?* It's meant to be a handbook for new peculiars—or people who've only just realized they're peculiar—but could also serve as a refresher for peculiars who haven't seen the inside of an ymbryne's classroom for many a year. It's an attempt to collect, for the first time in one place, all the information necessary for a peculiar to live in an unfriendly world. And for peculiars who have not had the benefit of an ymbryne's instruction, it will teach you something of our history, our customs, our secrets, our most famous and infamous members, and other general but essential knowledge.

That said, our world spans the globe, and there is much that even we ymbrynes still do not know about it. There are worlds yet to be discovered, even within our own. This is far from a complete and definitive guide; such a thing is impossible, unprintable; it would fill as many pages as there are grains of sand in the Sahara. I hope this introduction to peculiardom is merely a jumping-off point for your own explorations and discoveries, and that one day, Dear Reader, you will write a new chapter of your own.

Very peculiarly yours,
Alma LeFay Peregrine

Jacob, I wrote this book several years ago, so please understand if there are a few items which may now be out of date. In an attempt to correct the occasional obsolescence, and to highlight things which may be of special interest to you, I've written notes by hand here and there in the margins.

—Miss P

On
PECULIARS
and
PECULIARNESS

How vast is nature in its infinite varieties,
how inexhaustible in wonders! In its paradoxes our
greatest minds are baffled. In every strength is
hidden weakness; in every curse a hidden gift.

—FROM "THE MELANCHOLY TAXONOMIST" BY C. B. YARROWFORTH

The composition of the human species is infinitely more diverse than most humans suspect. The real taxonomy of Homo sapiens is a secret known to only a few. There are two branches: *coerlfolc*, the teeming mass of common people who make up humanity's great bulk, and the hidden branch—crypto-sapiens, if you will—who are called *syndrigast*, or "peculiar spirit" in the venerable language of our ancestors. And that is us.[1]

We peculiars are blessed with traits common people lack, as endless in combination and variety as birds are in the coloring of their feathers. These traits often skip a generation, or several, and as a result, peculiar children are rarely born to peculiar parents, and peculiar parents rarely produce peculiar children. This has prevented our kind from establishing

---

1. This address is adapted from *Standard Welcome Address for New Peculiars*, from the 1912 edition of *Screeds and Maxims*, approved by the Board of Declamations for use herein.

powerful familial dynasties, and instead produced a world in which many peculiar children are subjected to terrible abuse and neglect. It wasn't so many centuries ago that the parents of peculiars routinely assumed that their "real" child had been kidnapped and replaced by a changeling— the enchanted and malevolent offspring of fairies—which in darker times was considered a license to abandon the child, if not kill them outright. Happily, belief in fairies, witches, and the like is less common these days, so parents who discover their child levitating the family packhorse or projecting their voice into the mouth of a cat are more likely to assume they are hallucinating and seek psychiatric help than to fling the child down a well and burn their house to the ground, as was the old custom.

That doesn't mean the modern peculiar child's lot in life is an easy one. They are sure to feel alienated, confused, even frightened. Add to that the danger of being hunted by wights or hollowgast, especially if their ability is a strong one, and they are almost guaranteed to need an ymbryne's instruction at some point. Sadly, many peculiars never meet one.

This book is for them: the young peculiar (or the old one) who's never had the benefit of an ymbryne's guidance; who is lonely and filled with questions. The aim isn't merely to fill these pages with facts, stories, and advice. It also strives to hold up a mirror to peculiarness, so that in seeing some aspect of self named and described here—something which out of shame has been kept hidden from the world—peculiar children might feel understood, recognized, even proud. I know what it is to feel separate from a family that does not understand you, does not want you. I know what it is to feel absolutely alone: It is a withering torment. And I know, too, the saving grace of realizing for the first time that there are others like you.

Too many never do. This book's goal is to change that.

A Necessarily Incomplete Taxonomy of Peculiar Abilities

Newcomers and outsiders often confuse our peculiar traits with "superpowers" in the way that protagonists of comic book tales are endowed with superabilities like flight and extraordinary strength. But that is a vast oversimplification of the facts.

Peculiarness is complex, and peculiar abilities can confer both advantages and disadvantages. For every peculiar like Bronwyn Bruntley who has the strength of a "Captain Fantastick," there is another whose "power" is that she cannot stop sweating, ever, no matter how cold the climate (Cindy Keating, unkindly referred to as Perspirella Drench by her loopmates), or one who, rather than having a mouth between his chin and lips, has one embedded in the palm of his left hand and a corresponding trachea running up his arm (Raj Agarwal, about whom the phrase "talk to the hand" originated). But even these supposed afflictions have advantages—Raj can eat without silverware; Cindy is unaffected by extreme cold—and likewise, every perceived superability has its disadvantages. For example, my ward Emma Bloom can summon a ball of flame at her fingertips, but in her tender years she had to wear asbestos pajamas while she slept because she so often set her bed on fire. Millard Nullings's invisibility makes it possible for him to spy on others and easily avoid detection, but to achieve this he must be completely naked, which can be uncomfortable on chilly days and quite impossible in winter.

So as you can see—and, if you're reading this book, have no doubt experienced firsthand—we are not reducible to easy stereotypes. Peculiars are not superheroes, nor are we to be pitied. Instead, we occupy a vast spectrum. In every category there are exceptions, anomalies, and edge cases, not to mention that new peculiars with never-before-seen abilities are discovered every year.

The purpose of this list is to give a general impression of the breadth of our abilities and the most common categories into which they are classified, though it is by no means exhaustive. Nature bobs and weaves, and when we try to pin her down we only succeed in looking foolish. It would be futile to try and list every known peculiarness. That would require a book of its own, twice the length of the one you hold now.

····→ THE ELEMENTAL ABILITIES ←····

While these are some of the most spectacular and attention-grabbing peculiar talents, their prevalence is overstated. Perhaps one out of ten can claim some elemental ability, and those do not always fall neatly into categories. For instance, I knew a young lady who could only manipulate mud (a combination of water and earth talents). There was a boy who ate compost and lived his whole life in the garden—because he was rooted there, quite literally, by arterial roots that sprouted from his feet and ran deep into the earth. Can we call this boy an earthworker? He didn't manipulate the earth; if anything, it was the earth that worked *him*. But how else to categorize him? So, you see, these classifications are useful only to a point, and even when we try to sub-classify and *sub*-sub-classify, the lines we so painstakingly draw are quickly blurred. And yet, the attempt must be made.

Daisies grew in a trail behind her feet.

EARTHWORKERS

Some earthworkers are able to excavate large holes in the ground with a flick of the wrist, or ride waves of sand across a landscape of dunes. Others use the earth as a medium to manipulate things that grow within it, like my ward Fiona Frauenfeld, who can make plants grow with astonishing speed. Desdemona Frump, pictured left, was trailed everywhere by daisies, which sprang up behind her as she walked.

FIRE-STARTERS, AKA "SPARKS"

A fire-starter can summon fire with their hands (like Emma Bloom), or with their toes, or can breathe fire from their mouths, like the performer who called himself the Human Volcano (pictured). One infamous fire-starter could shoot flames from his nether regions as far as thirty feet. I will leave the details to your imagination.

Edge case: A peculiar boy named Ham Peggotty had the ability to extinguish flames with his saliva, which he produced in prodigious volumes.

He called himself the Human Volcano.

GALVANIZERS

These peculiars have such an excess of electricity flowing through them that they can power lightbulbs with just a touch of their finger. The most gifted can call lightning down from the skies. Others, like Slemina Gray, have bodies that act like batteries, and can provide backup power during outages. It's also been observed that radio transmissions are stronger and clearer in her presence.

Slemina Gray, human battery

A glaciator's home . . . in summer.

GLACIATORS

The best known of the bunch, Althea G. is a powerful young woman whose ability to shape and create ice is astonishing. She can create giant ice sculptures, summon snow and hail, and freeze people, animals, and buildings with a touch.

Her heart, it seems, is unaffected by this cold; she is known for her kindness toward animals and young children, her loyalty to friends, and her sentimental poetry.

12

Althea G., the famous glaciator.

May she rest in peace. She gave her life protecting the Ymbryne Council from an enemy assault, having frozen the interior into a maze of solid ice.

A water-tamer at work.

WATER-TAMERS AND RAINMAKERS

Water-tamers have long found careers in the seagoing trades. Their ability to summon currents and waves can guide whole schools of fish into nets, speed sailing ships through calm and windless conditions, steer sailors away from dangerous rocks—or directly toward them. Rainmakers, their elemental cousins, are so revered by farmers that some have lived openly in small agrarian communities among normals for years, protected as if they were sacred talismans.

Noted example: The title character of "The Boy Who Could Hold Back the Sea" from *Tales of the Peculiar.*

Edge case: Latoya Smith could make the sky rain grasshoppers, and was responsible for several entomological weather events that normals interpreted as presaging a biblical apocalypse.

Water-tamer Roy Chao got carried away . . . and so did his house.

····⇥ LIGHT-SHAPERS ⇤····

Considered cousins to the elementals, light-shapers can take light from the air with their hands and redirect it. One young man, a ward of Miss Yippin's named Julius, might properly be called a light-*eater*, or a phosphagist, as his talent involves devouring the light and storing it inside his body for future use.

A phosphagous light-shaper about to eat her elevenses.

····⇥ ZEPHYRS ⇤····

Variously known as cloud-bankers, air-walkers, gusters, and *cumulae*, these elementals can manipulate air and clouds to great effect. The zephyr catchall encompasses a wide spectrum of sub-talents that ranges from commanding great gusts of wind and the formation of clouds to levitation. Those of us who are lighter than air, like my ward Olive Abroholos Elephanta, are also classed among the zephyrs.

Edge case: The peculiar American Angelica Minervis is pursued everywhere by a dark cloud emanating from her ear canal. She can make the cloud rain, snow, or hail anytime she likes. Thus she is equal parts zephyr, rainmaker, and glaciator.

Angelica: a bit of this, a bit of that.

A light-shaper practicing her craft.

As you know, we've lately met
a number of light-shapers!
Feel free to annotate this book
yourself. Jacob ...

····→ THE MORPHOLOGICAL ABILITIES ←····

The "morphos," as they're sometimes called, are gifted with peculiarity of form. Some can effect remarkable change upon their own bodies (shape-shifters, for example), while others maintain a constant form that is nevertheless remarkably unique (invisibles, dissocios).

INVISIBLES

Millard Nullings is only the most famous of the invisibles; there are many others. They are sometimes forgotten, however, because they are so easily overlooked. Invisibles generally begin disappearing just before puberty, and the process is gradual, commencing with the toes and working upward until the entire body vanishes. Some wrap themselves in layers of clothing to hide any exposed skin. Others, finding this tedious and humiliating (not to mention hot in summer), simply disappear and live their lives

An invisible poses nude in a photo studio.

naked and alone. Those fortunate enough to be discovered by ymbrynes often blossom into scholars. Because conversations can be challenging when others cannot read your facial expressions, many retreat into the world of books.

THE ANATOMICALLY UNIQUE

The human body expresses itself in an astonishing array of forms—which is entirely normal. There is nothing peculiar, ipso facto, about being extremely tall, or small, or rotund, or having more or fewer limbs than is standard, etc. To qualify as peculiar—and to then, therefore, possess that seed of peculiar soul that grants one entrance to time loops—there must

Sergei Andropov could jelly his joints at will, making them bendable to the extreme.

be some additional feature that would be impossible in a normal person. Dissocios, for instance, can remove their heads from their bodies for several hours and then reattach them with no medical consequences. My ward Claire Densmore has a second mouth filled with sharp teeth in the back of her head; it is connected to her stomach via a second throat. (I also heard it speak, once, while she was asleep, in Latin. I believe it may also be connected to a small second brain hidden somewhere inside her body.) Peculiar contortionists are not just flexible; they can liquefy their bones at will in order to tuck themselves into the unlikeliest of spaces. Sometimes the true peculiarity of a morphologically unique person is hidden, or unknown even to them, but that is of no importance. Anyone with a peculiar soul is welcome among us.

SHAPE-SHIFTERS

As a general rule, only ymbrynes can shape-shift, and only from human to bird form and contrariwise. Exceptions to this rule are so vanishingly rare that only one has been seen in my lifetime: a Frenchman named Hallonde who could change himself into a dog. He spent much of his waking life in canine form, claiming that he slept better as a dog, and that to eat as a dog was an exceptional joy, as it made even the lowliest scraps into *cuisine gastronomique.*

Mssr. Hallonde at table.

····→ ABILITIES OF STRENGTH ←····

In the peculiar world, strength expresses itself in two forms: that of body and that of mind. Allow me to elucidate the difference.

THE FORTAE

Quite a few peculiars can boast incredible strength of body, like my beloved ward Bronwyn Bruntley and her late brother, Victor. Bronwyn's talent has an advantage over some less fortunate fortae, in that she can moderate her power when handling delicate objects and people. Those who cannot face practical challenges: They can only drink from cups made of stone, cannot hold a pen to write their name, and cannot embrace their loved ones for fear of crushing them to death.

Victor Bruntley, Bronwyn's late brother.

Derwitt Vanderflunke could launch ships with just his hands, but could not hug his mother.

TELEKINETICS

These peculiars' strength is mental and can be projected across distances by non-physical means.

There are many among us. Melina Manon of Miss Thrush's loop is one. This promising young woman, employed at the Peculiar Archives, can shift heavy objects using only her mind. It's said that the leader of the American Californio clan, J. M. Parkins, can levitate his own wheelchair.

Roberto Popplin, known to his public as "The Great Teleki-neato."

····➔ PECULIAR COMMUNICATORS ◆····

ANIMAL COMMUNICATORS

These peculiars are gifted with the ability to intercourse with everyday beasts and insects. A few can make themselves understood while speaking in a human tongue such as English, but most have learned to use the animals' preferred method of communication. Abed Rahman can perfectly reproduce the bleatings of deer, and they surround him whenever he walks through the woods. He also has hooves instead of feet and will turn and flee at the slightest startling noise, leading us to believe he is part deer himself. Polymorphism is no prerequisite, however: I know of peculiars who are covered in dog fur but cannot communicate with dogs, and yet the Canadian peculiar Jolene Foy, who has no canine features at all, can make herself understood by them with a seemingly infinite variety of barks, growls, and high-pitched whines.

The animal communicator's method need not even be verbal. Hugh Apiston's control over the bees that live inside his stomach is entirely mental, though he also employs a few hand gestures when commanding them.

Lillian Link claimed she never met anyone more articulate than her snake.

Further, many ymbrynes can and do communicate with their own species of bird. I, for instance, can hold long conversations with peregrines and other closely related species of falcon, though I've found, disappointingly, that most of them are only interested in talking about food.

These are only a few examples. There are also peculiars who've demonstrated the ability to communicate with whole colonies of ants and scorpions, all manner of the order Rodentia, turtles, warm-blooded fish, horses, cows, wolves, and on and on.

For an account of peculiar animals, which is an altogether different matter, please turn to the next section: Peculiar Animals and Plants.

MENTALISTS

Mentalists communicate using only their minds. Some can hold entire conversations without ever opening their mouths (or signing with their hands), while others, like my ward Horace Somnusson, communicate with the future via trances and dreams. (Horace has described his prophecies as films that play in his head, but also as a bodiless dream-voice speaking to him from he knows not where.) A few psychically talented peculiars can read thoughts. Bernard Bagstock was one, and his was a lonely life. Though his intentions were good, people were

Mentalist in a trance.

Merrill's dreams were only prophetic if she napped atop the haystack.

so afraid to have their thoughts invaded that they steered well clear of him, and he left peculiar society to live as a hermit in the woods.

A notable sub-classification of mentalists are dreamworkers, who can take the stuff of dreams, render it physical, remove it from the brain, and then do all manner of things with it. (For a diverting story about one such person, you might read "The Girl Who Could Tame Nightmares" in *Tales of the Peculiar*.)

Edge case: While some ymbrynes consider diviners a type of mentalist, I class them in a category by themselves. In my opinion, while some have talents that border on premonition and prophecy, divining is more a heightened sensitivity of body than of mind. Water diviners are pulled toward underground springs in a manner that's quite physical. Loop diviners describe feeling a "gravitational surge" when close to a loop entrance. And so on.

What Eugenia Brody could divine, she would never say. But she would often stand for hours outside a house where some tragedy had occurred, whispering.

PLANT COMMUNICATORS

A vanishingly small number of peculiars can speak to plants, and a smaller number still can understand the plants' replies. There is much to be learned from plants, I'm told, and especially from trees, some of whom are the oldest living things on Earth. I once knew a tree-talker named Sweedlepipe who would lecture anyone within earshot about the indignity of having one's friends turned into lumber and toilet tissue. He was convicted of murdering a lumberjack, rescued from the hangman's noose by Miss Avocet, and exiled to a treeless island loop in the Far North.

Young tree-talkers posing with their beloved pet twigs.

SPIRITISTS

As contrasted with mentalists, who communicate with the living using only their minds, spiritists are able to communicate with the dead. Some use well-established methods like Ouija boards or the séance table, while others employ more unorthodox tools, such as the telephone. I knew of one young man who wrote letters to the deceased in microscopic handwriting and packed them into tiny capsules of undigestible plastic. When they later emerged, a day or so hence, the letters would be answered.

Mae and Jane could talk to the dead, but only if they phoned ahead.

····➤ THE NECROLOGICALLY GIFTED ◀····

DEADRISERS

These curious peculiars can reanimate lifeless tissue using organs harvested from the dead. Enoch O'Connor, my ward and a typical (if at times frustrating) example, uses hearts and brains preserved in pickling jars to wake the dead for brief periods of time. He can also galvanize small inanimate objects, creating armies of miniature homunculi which invariably cause mischief.

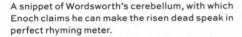

A snippet of Wordsworth's cerebellum, with which Enoch claims he can make the risen dead speak in perfect rhyming meter.

Enoch wasted half a dozen hearts teaching old Susie to play piano.

Edge case: Some ymbrynes insist that the Librarians of Abaton fall under this banner, too, since they are the only peculiars who can access souls once they're deposited into soul jars (and even "read" them, according to ancient accounts). It's my opinion that the Librarians' talents are poorly understood and extend far beyond necrology.

After all, we know now that you are one, and you can do much more than empty soul jars. I wonder if you have any more hidden talents waiting to reveal themselves ···

BONE-MENDERS

It may seem counterintuitive to include our healers among the necrologically gifted, but their life-preserving talents are always paired with an aptitude for the mortal arts. Their medicines are derived and distilled from the dead, and half their gift is in transmuting the hearts and humours of the deceased into miraculous elixirs. In the midst of life we are in death, *et cetera*.

Regrettably, bone-mending is an exceedingly rare talent. Were it more common, the Ymbryne Council would mandate that every loop in peculiardom include a bonemender. While they are not a perfect replacement for the care of a trained medical doctor, there is much that a bone-mender can do that a normal doctor cannot, for they specialize in maladies and injuries of the peculiar sort. No one else can calm a fever caused by an infected hollowgast bite. No garden-variety physician could be trusted to treat the sudden and spontaneous growth of a second head, much less a third. My own longtime mender, Rafael, has become famous for his unusually potent tinctures and poultices, which have cured several peculiar diseases previously thought fatal, like brain-cranny worms and the dreaded Siberian semi-sentient psoriasis. It's a shame we don't have more of them.

Bone-mender W. H. Schmidt's calling card.

There also exist self-healers, who can speedily recover from grievous injuries with no medical intervention, but whose talents do not, unfortunately, extend beyond themselves. The rarest manifestation of the bone-mending talent are so-called dust people, whose skin and bone can be ground into healing powders. The powder's efficacy is nothing short of miraculous when applied to the wounds of others, but has no effect at all upon the donor.

FIELD DISPATCH BY A. PORTMAN
OF A BONE-MENDER LIVING AMONG NORMALS
IN FLORIDA:

George had been the town doctor for as long as anyone could remember. He ministered to the aches and ailments of rich and poor alike, and was remembered for his gentleness and his otherworldly intuition. Long before X-rays were common in these parts, he seemed able to look inside people without needing a knife, and when he cut out Gracie Cohunk's cancer, he knew right where to find it on the first cut. No one knew how he did it, and no one asked. Neither did they ask how old he was, though the oldest people in town had foggy recollections of Old George cooling fevers and patching bones even when they were tykes.

George only performed house calls, and no one had ever called on him at his home, which he'd fashioned from the sleeping car of an old circus train—though he had never, to anyone's knowledge, been in the circus. A local boy claimed to have snuck into George's train car when the doctor wasn't at home. He said there was nothing in it at all: not a dish, not a stick of furniture. Only a carpet of dust as thick as a slab of country ham.

Old George the bone-mender.

Peculiar Animals
and Plants

····➔ PECULIAR ANIMALS ⬅····

At one time, millennia ago, peculiar animals thrived. There were more peculiar animals in the world than there were peculiar people, and they came in an astonishing diversity of forms: whales that could fly like birds, worms as big as houses, dogs of true genius (rather than just affected genius). It is one of the great tragedies of our age that their numbers have been so reduced. Not only have peculiar animals long been prized by trophy hunters, but the very intelligent among them were routinely suspected of being possessed by demons and subjected to the same persecutions peculiar humans have suffered. (For a comprehensive analysis, see *The Criminal Prosecution and Capital Punishment of Animals* by E. P. Ewans, which lists in detail the criminal trials, incarcerations, and campaigns of retributive butchery waged upon species including moles, oxen, pigs, dogs, sparrows, and even dolphins over the centuries.) Needless to say, after millennia of mistreatment they have been pushed to the brink of survival, and only a small number are left today. Most peculiar children have never met one. Those that remain live in small, well-hidden menagerie loops, like the one overseen by Miss Wren.✳

One exception to this rule of scarcity is the venerable grimbear. Strong enough to fight off a hollowgast, but so gentle they're entrusted with the care of children, these fearsome, intelligent animals have long been the

✳ *Now it's up to us all to protect them however we can——.*

A grimbear and her young charges.

preferred companions of ymbrynes in northern climes, where grimbear training is an old and respected art.

The *pullum periculum*, popularly known as the Armageddon chicken, lays explosive eggs. It's a defense mechanism that's very effective at deterring animal predators from raiding their nests, but when humans discovered their eggs could be used as weapons, these chickens became highly sought-after. Hannibal carried a whole flock with him in his campaign against the Romans in 218 BC, along with herds of war elephants and the eighteen-tusked wildebeest Ca'ab Magda. But the chickens fare poorly in captivity and nearly went extinct. There are only a few known flocks left in the world.

A brave woman with her explosive chicken.

Peculiar animals are sometimes discovered languishing in circus sideshows, where they are invariably depressed, dressed in humiliating clothes, and forced to perform shallow feats of intellect for audiences. Miss Wren personally emancipated over a hundred animals from sideshows and circuses, including Mook-Mook, the macaque shown below, pictured shortly before his rescue. He went on to distinguish himself in the field of mathematics, solving both the infamous Hodge Conjecture and the Reimann Hypothesis. In both cases he was denied the $1,000,000 prize on offer because journals refused to publish the work of a monkey.

With the aid of a secretary, this tortoise authored fifteen novels under the pseudonym T. Leatherback. His thrillers were panned for their sluggish pace, but his two forays into romance have become classics of the genre.

When intelligent peculiar animals mass in great numbers, as happened occasionally in ancient times, they tended to replicate the struggles and strife of human beings. In the thirteenth century, opposing schools of peculiar fish had a territorial dispute that led to outright war. Matthew of Paris, a monk and chronicler of the thirteenth century, tells the tale in his *Historia Anglorum*:

Mook-Mook can juggle five balls and hop on one leg, and he solved the infamous Hodge Conjecture in mathematics.

Although other great and unheard-of wonders happened in this year [1240], we have thought it worth our while to mention in this work one more remarkable than the rest. As it is the nature of the sea to vomit up on dry land the dead bodies thrown into it, about eleven whales, besides other marine monsters, were cast up on the seacoast of England, dead, as if they had been injured in some kind of struggle—not, however, by the attacks or skill of man. The sailors and old people dwelling near the coast, who had seen the wonders of the deep when following their vocation in the vast waters and trafficking to distant countries, declared that there had been an unusual battle amongst the fishes, beasts, and monsters of the deep, which by wounding and gnawing each other, had caused death to several; and the dead had been cast ashore.

While we have no further evidence that such a battle took place, we neither have reason to doubt Matthew's account, as such battles had happened before.

····➔ PECULIAR PLANTS ◆····

Though a little-known phenomenon, there are a few documented examples of peculiar flora: seemingly sentient, even intelligent, plants. There was a lingonberry bush in Slough which could answer simple yes-or-no questions by shaking its leaves, and a cabbage in Cork that ate the farmer who grew it. There was the famous case of the gourd with a heartbeat—and thus, it was determined, a heart—and the man who fell in love with it. I won't rehash their story here, as it was written about ad nauseam in that execrable tabloid, the *Muckraker*, but I'm told they retired to a cottage in the Forest of Dean and are very happy.

Moments before he was eaten by his own cabbage.

EMINENT FIGURES FROM HISTORY
YOU MIGHT NOT HAVE REALIZED WERE PECULIAR

O pen any history book and point to a list of famous names; most likely one of them is peculiar. Many of us have left an indelible mark upon wider society, especially those who were blessed with both prodigious talent and a gift for passing as normal. As a peculiar, you have much to be proud of—the great achievements of humankind are ours, too, and would not have been possible without us. Unfortunately, the most celebrated peculiars in history were also the most adept at keeping their true natures hidden, for exposure meant ruin, both of life and reputation. Thus, the only names we can be certain of are those whose peculiarness was at best a poorly kept secret, and so by its very nature this list is merely a sampling, by no means authoritative or complete. As for the rest, you will have to satisfy yourself with guessing at their identities. Cleopatra? Shakespeare? Harry Houdini? Stephen Hawking? Perhaps, perhaps. Even in our supposedly enlightened age, most of us must still tread in the shadows or risk terrible consequences.

ISAMBARD KINGDOM BRUNEL, b. 1806, was one of Britain's great engineers, having contributed materially to the development of new types of bridges, tunnels, and ships. He also had unbreakable bones, which he discovered after surviving several dramatic worksite disasters—falls from great heights, tunnel cave-ins, etc.—which would have killed a normal man. Wrongly convinced he was immortal, Brunel devised a harebrained system of travel which involved being sucked through long pneumatic tubes underground. He was about to test it when an unrelated accident put him in hospital: While amusing his children with a conjuring trick,

Brunel had unbreakable bones but was nearly killed by a half-sovereign coin.

he inhaled a half-sovereign coin, which was only dislodged after six weeks and many attempts. In his later years he told the story of being strapped to a board, inverted, and shaken like a rag doll until finally he heard the gold piece strike the back of his teeth, which he called "the most exquisite moment of my life." Cured of the idea that he was unkillable, Brunel took better care of himself from then on, only to die of a kidney disorder at the tender age of fifty-three. He donated his femur bones to the Peculiar Archives, where visitors are welcome to try and shatter them by any means available.

After **ISABELLA BIRD**, b. 1831, flunked out of the Ymbryne Academy in 1849, she embarked upon a life of near-constant travel. Her goal was to map and document as many distant loops and make contact with as many far-flung ymbrynes as she could, reasoning that if she could not become a full-fledged ymbryne with a loop to call her own, she could at least act as an ambassador. She was welcomed in loops from Hawaii to Tibet, though her travels nearly came to an end when she fell in love with a one-eyed fron-

Miss Isabella Bird.

tiersman in Colorado named Rocky Mountain Jim. Her expeditions established lines of communication between our own Ymbryne Council and loops around the world, though these ties were mostly severed after the emergence of the hollowgast in 1908.

SIR ARTHUR CONAN DOYLE, b. 1859, wasn't just the author of the Sherlock Holmes stories (a character who certainly would have been peculiar, had he been real). Conan Doyle was also an ardent spiritist with a peculiar "second sight" that allowed him to peer, on occasion, beyond the veil of death. His ability was heightened by the trauma of the Great War, which claimed one of his sons. He wrote books on the topic, held séances, experimented with telepathy, sat with mediums, professed to believe in fairies, and was a celebrated member of a group of London supernaturalists called the Ghost Club, which counted among its number several peculiars. It's rumored that he lived out his later years in a loop in Sussex, but he fastidiously hid his knowledge of peculiardom from the normal world, for fear of the harm that publicity would bring us.

This medal depicts the eccentric bibliophile surrounded by books. His motto: "Our knowledge consists of what we remember."

ANTONIO MAGLIABECHI, b. 1633, was gifted with perfect recall and a photographic memory—as well as a great number of eccentric habits. He was, first and foremost, an obsessive bibliomaniac. He saw no use in cleaning his house or even changing his clothes, "life being so short and books so plentiful." He was regarded as a living encyclopedia, and scholars would often consult him while researching any number of topics. Asking Magliabechi a question was a bit like searching the "world wide web" these days. His house was so crowded with books, not only on shelves but piled in heaps on the floor, that it was difficult to walk from one room to another. To keep his hands warm as he read, he had a small stove fastened to his forearms, which left his clothes singed and begrimed with soot. He sat reading all day in a sort of wooden cradle, which was connected to the surrounding book-heaps by nets of spiderwebs he would never allow to be cleared away. He considered the webs, and the colony of spiders who created them, his dear friends.

Lord Francis dining with his beloved dogs.

The third Duke of Bridgewater, **FRANCIS EGERTON,** b. 1736, is credited with building the world's first modern canal, which he named after himself, but is better known among peculiars as one of our foremost animal communicators. He could speak with dogs, and by all accounts preferred their company to that of humans. Egerton dined with his dogs, dressed them in tailor-made formal clothes, and threw them lavish parties. They were even allowed use of the Duke's carriages, and were often driven around town by his chauffeurs.

LEONARDO DA VINCI, b. 1452, wasn't peculiar, but he was nevertheless mentored by an ymbryne as a child, and for the rest of his life he would buy caged birds only to set them free. It's thought that his ymbryne governess was the real subject of his most famous painting, the *Mona Lisa*.

My ancestor's mummy has become the unofficial mascot of a London university.

JEREMY BENTHAM, b. 1748, was an ancestor of mine; I am almost certainly the inheritor of his peculiar genes. My brother Myron took his last name as a tribute to old Uncle Jeremy, as we called him; though, to his chagrin, Myron was never as brilliant as our forebear. The original Bentham was an influential philosopher and writer whose best-known contribution to society was the concept of moral utilitarianism, which holds that an action is right if it creates happiness in the greatest number of people, notwithstanding the suffering of a few. (By which logic, nothing my brother Caul ever did was right.) Uncle Jeremy also devised a prison based on the idea that prisoners (and society as a whole) will behave if they believe they are always being watched. He called this theoretical prison the Panopticon, a name Myron borrowed for his loop device. In this same spirit of surveillance, Jeremy specified in his will that after death he should be mummified and his body placed, fully dressed with hat and cane, in a glass cabinet in the hallway of University College London, where the students and faculty of his most beloved institution might always feel the weight of his gaze. You can find his mummified "auto-icon" there still, looking only slightly the worse for wear given that he died nearly two centuries ago. As for his peculiar talent, old Uncle Jeremy kept it a closely held secret, though he was most assuredly peculiar; he was a regular presence in our London loops and was even allowed to attend Ymbryne Council meetings as a nonvoting observer. He is occasionally still present at our meetings, his mummy secreted out of its case at the university and placed at the edge of the Council Chamber once every decade or so, where he is noted on the roll.

Mary Seacole as pictured on the cover of her autobiography.

MARY SEACOLE, b. 1805, was a British-Jamaican nurse, an enterprising businesswoman, an author, and a hero of the Crimean War whose hygienic methods predated, and may have inspired, those of Florence Nightingale. (They certainly saved many lives.) Those who knew she was peculiar assumed she was a bone-mender, due to her tremendous skill in the treatment of sickness, when in fact she was an ymbryne. Many of the boardinghouses she ran in the course of her world travels were also loops, and during the bloody Crimean conflict she cared for both peculiar children inside her loop and wounded soldiers outside it. I never had the pleasure of meeting her, but stories of her ambition, industry, and kindness inspired a generation of young ymbrynes.

A SHORT LIST OF PEOPLE WHO WERE PROBABLY PECULIAR,
THOUGH NO DEFINITIVE PROOF EXISTS:

» **SALVADOR DALÍ** «

» **P. T. BARNUM** «

» **BOUDICCA** «

» **ENGLISHMAN "MAD JACK" FULLER,** «
who was buried beneath a pyramid of his own construction, seated
upright at a table with a roast chicken and a bottle of claret.

» **VINCENT VAN GOGH** «

» **JOAN** OF **ARC** «

» **GEORGE WASHINGTON CARVER** «

» **OSCAR WILDE** «

» **ARCHIMEDES** «

» **SIR WALTER RALEIGH** «

» **THE SECOND BARONESS** OF **WALLINGFORD,** «
who was such a recluse that she had an extensive series of tunnels
built beneath her estate so that she might go from place to place
without being observed.

» **NIKOLA TESLA** «

TIME LOOPS

> "Time loops are like grimbears. Attend to them with gentleness and constancy and they'll protect you forever. Neglect them and they'll kill you in a flash."
>
> —ESMERELDA AVOCET

In ancient times people mistook us for gods, but we peculiars are no less mortal than common folk. Time loops merely delay the inevitable, and the price we pay for using them is hefty—an irrevocable divorce from the ongoing present. Long-term loop dwellers can but dip their toes into the now lest they wither and die. This has been the arrangement since time immemorial.

If you're reading this book, you will surely be familiar with the basic concept of the time loop, though it's possible you may not have encountered one yet. All peculiars should have a good working knowledge of time loops. For thousands of years they have been our saving grace, and will assuredly be so again. Despite many attempts to purge us from the earth, their refuge has always ensured our survival. They provide us homes where we can live openly as peculiars without fear of repression or reprisal. Without them we would still be born, and live, but

Miss Bramblebash and friends in front of their loop exit at the precise moment of reset.

it would be a cowering, scurrying sort of life. Those able to hide their abilities would be forced to forever deny their true natures and rarely know the comfort of another peculiar's company. Those too peculiar to hide it would live perpetually in the shadows, or be subjected to the deprivations of prison, or the asylum, or disfiguring "corrective" surgeries.

All of which is to say: loops are a miracle that have spared us from many hells, and as such we owe them our respect and a bit of scholarly attention.

Time loops come in many shapes and sizes. They are dispersed throughout the world wherever there are ymbrynes, who are their makers and maintainers. We know the locations of only a small fraction of these, and I cannot print a map of them here for fear that this volume may fall into unfriendly hands. But if you are a peculiar badly in need of finding one, this guide may aid in your search. What's more: I believe that peculiars and loops create between them a kind of mutual magnetism, not unlike a dowser using a divining rod to search for underground rivers. Seek and ye shall find, or at any rate you may draw near enough that any ymbryne worth her wings will be able to find you scratching about the keyhole and usher you inside.

A rather inconvenient loop entrance.

⤙ THE CARE AND FEEDING ⤚
OF TIME LOOPS

A time loop repeats a twenty-four hour period indefinitely, for as long as an ymbryne performs her daily reset. (There are a few rare loops that don't require a daily reset, but more on those happy unicorns later.) These resets vary in technique and complexity, and are generally performed by the same ymbryne who created the loop, but not always. Any ymbryne can reset any loop, and in some regions that once had ymbrynes but currently lack them—notably, America—loops can be maintained by demi-ymbrynes and clock-winders (aka "loop-keepers"), though their work is sometimes shoddy and can result in loop shift and other unwanted and dangerous degradations of a loop's temporal fabric.

This twenty-four-hour period—the twenty-four hours prior to the loop's creation—is set in stone the moment the ymbryne creates the loop. This period is nearly impossible to change. It is thus very important for the ymbryne to choose the day carefully, taking into account factors like weather, location, and the behavior of normals inside the looped zone. No one wants to live forever in a frosty, sunless winter day. Likewise to be avoided are days when floods, fires, or other natural disasters bedevil the area. Lastly, most loops are centered around large houses where the ymbryne's wards can live, and if the area immediately surrounding the house is free of normals for the entire twenty-four-hour period—or of meddlesome ones, at any rate—all the better. If a group of easily frightened normal schoolchildren parade through the back garden every afternoon, that is an annoyance which will have to be dealt with for eternity.

Of course, not all ymbrynes are able to choose the time and location of their loops. Many loops are made in emergency situations, when an enemy is closing in, for instance, or some disaster is about to strike and evacuating your wards to another place isn't practical or possible. My loop, for instance, was created during an aerial bombardment. If I had waited a moment longer, the house would've been destroyed and my peculiar wards with it. And while it's possible to adjust the looped period down the road—by leaving the loop, allowing it to lapse, and then returning to remake it on a better day—it's rarely worth the risk, especially when there are enemies about.

····→ TIME LOOPS: an ANATOMY ←····

I n very general terms, the average time loop is approximately a kilometer wide. Many are smaller (some as small as a house, or in the case of pocket loops, a garden shed) and some are larger, but a kilometer is a reasonably average width. That gives the loop's inhabitants a bit of room to spread out and exercise their legs now and then, which helps prevent both madness and stiffness of the extremities, but it is not so much room that they are likely to get lost.

OPEN LOOP   **CLOSED LOOP**

Loops are egg-shaped, their boundaries resembling the elliptical orbit of a planet around a star. Those boundaries extend in all directions, including up and down. If you were to dig a half kilometer into the earth beneath the center of a loop, you would encounter its bottom edge.[2] The boundary is hard but invisible, and many a reckless peculiar child has been hurt by running straight into one at full tilt.

Loops can be open or closed to the outer past. A closed loop has no exit but to the present. An open loop has, hidden somewhere in its boundary membrane, an exit point to the past, which is distinct from its exit

---

2. A prisoner with molelike forepaws once tried to escape a punishment loop in this fashion, digging straight down, though all he accomplished was to nearly drown in a muddy hole when he hit the water table.

My own loop's boundaries and environs. If you squint and peer closely
you can almost see Emma standing on the colonnaded porch of our house.

into the present. This opening leads into the wider world of the looped
day, which presents exciting opportunities to explore broad swaths of the
past. The outer past does not loop, of course, and the days will tick by as
they do in the present. But there are still many dangers, not least of which
is that you may easily become lost.

The temptation to right historical wrongs or avert past disasters has
ensnared many a well-meaning peculiar. Be warned: The past cannot be
changed. History heals itself. Even so, some foolish peculiars still embark
on quixotic quests to assassinate murderous dictators or prevent doomed
ships from leaving port; this may provide short-term satisfaction, but in
the end nothing is achieved. Beware the temptation to grasp at this fleeting form of glory. The past will erase your achievements, and, more often
than not, you along with them.

Others have been tempted to flee into the past to escape their trou-
bles, but the unlooped outer past is an unwelcoming place. It does
not want us there; the work of repairing the damage we do to history

simply by walking down the street is huge, and after some months, the past's natural immune system seems to decide that eliminating the interloper is easier than constantly cleaning up the temporal messes we leave behind. If you must travel through the unlooped past, our official recommendation is that you limit your journey to four weeks at the maximum.

PERMALOOPS are a rare loop variant that require only infrequent resets. Very few ymbrynes have been able to create a permaloop (though many have tried), and even those powerful enough to do so once have never been able to make another. Permaloops were more common a thousand years ago. Fewer than five are known to exist today, and all are small. This is because there is a direct correlation between the size of a loop and the difficulty of maintaining it: A large loop requires more skill and ymbrynic ability to sustain than a small one. Kilometer-wide permaloops are unheard of.

The most famous permaloop still operational lies in a sewer tunnel beneath Waterloo, Iowa, where a dinner for four hundred people is held every night on the world's longest banquet table. The loop was

Waterloo, Iowa sewer tunnel permaloop, 1903.

Miss Ginny
Quetzal,
looking
somewhat
chagrined.

created while the city was celebrating its new sewer, and in attendance
that night was an ymbryne named Ginny Quetzal. She was so taken
with the scene and the event that she created a loop there and then, that
she might enjoy it all again the following evening, and the one after
that. She had no idea she'd made a permanent loop until she returned
a year later to find the banquet still ongoing. (Some ymbrynes don't
know their own power.) Miss Quetzal has long bemoaned that she created such a special loop by accident, and in such a silly place. Still, if
you're ever in Waterloo, Iowa, you might pry up the manhole cover at
the corner of Randolph and Wellington and pop down for a free meal.
Formalwear is a must.

POCKET LOOPS must be reset every month or so, but they are too small to be lived in, usually just a few meters square. They are also a fairly recent phenomenon, invented to create points of contact with Myron Bentham's Panloopticon device. They aren't refuges, but nodes of transport.

Peculiardom's most well-known pocket loop is surely the one I created in the backyard of your parents' home, in the garden shed. If you could provide a photo, I'd like to include it in future editions of this book. Please do apologize to your mother and father on my behalf for its destruction——

····➔ WHICH LOOP SHOULD I LIVE IN? ◄····
A FLOWING CHART

Among an ymbryne's many responsibilities, maintaining a harmonious balance of personalities within our loops is of the utmost importance. Because it's nearly impossible to improve the minds of one's wards when they are fighting like wet cats, we try to consider personality when selecting new additions, and the proclivities and sensitivities of the prospective new member, too; some children simply do not adapt well to certain eras or areas of the world,[3] or cannot get along with

---

3. I was once sent a ward by Miss Avocet, a glum young man named Salvador Tatterleg, who had grown up in the sunny climes of Andalusia. He refused to wear anything but short pants and could not accustom himself to our colder weather or our "strange" food. (It was jellied calf trotter night, I remember, when

certain others.[4] The ymbryne is creating an ersatz family, after all, and her role is akin to that of a matchmaker. But even ymbrynes can misjudge people, and conflicts may arise despite careful consideration of personality and temperament. Moreover, new adoptees might feel out of place for reasons that cannot be anticipated in advance, such as the quirks of a particular loop day. Miss Firecrown once had a ward who couldn't stand the mating shriek of the Madagascan aye-aye, and it happened that at exactly 3:20 in the afternoon each day a whole squad of them went about their lustful pursuits in the forest near Miss Firecrown's house. The ward in question braved it out for nearly ten years, but finally was driven to distraction by it and requested a transfer to another loop.

These things happen on occasion. Living in a loop is a privilege, not a jail sentence. If you have a compelling reason why you can no longer live in your assigned loop, you may submit a written request for transfer to the Undersecretary of Inter-loop Affairs, Peculiar Children Office, Lamentations Dept. If the Undersecretary deems your reasons well-grounded, she will pass the request to the Reviewing Committee for the Office of Quibbles and Grousing, then to the Ombudswoman in Charge of Brushing Off Bothersome Requests, after which it may come before the Ymbryne Council. You may then be asked which loop you would prefer to live in. Since loop transfer requests are rarely granted more than once per ward per lifetime, you should consider your options carefully in advance.

We've designed the following chart to aid your decision-making. It is not, of course, comprehensive; there are many more loops in the world than are listed here. But it will give you an idea of the many diverse factors you should take into account when considering a change. Upon reflection, you may decide to stay right where you are.

---

he stopped taking dinner altogether.) Worse, he fell in love with my ward Fiona Frauenfeld nearly upon arrival, and though Fiona made it plain she did not return his affections, he could not stop mooning after her. This earned him the opprobrium of Hugh, her longtime paramour, and the two were at each other's throats most days. Finally (perhaps inevitably), Salvador attempted to run away. I found him in a leaky rowboat a great distance from our island, bee-stung and staring at the sky in a heartbroken daze, surrounded by eel sandwiches, which was all he'd been able to purloin from our kitchens. I brought him back to shore and put in an official request for transfer, and Miss Avocet found him a warmer, less-frequently-bombed loop to live in, where he could recover from the sting of his spurned advances (and Hugh's bees).

4. For instance, an old rule of thumb is never to place a fire-starter and a glaciator together in the same loop; their abilities, ardors, and personalities all tend to be strongly in opposition, and they will clash to the point of mutual exhaustion.

WHICH LOOP SHOULD I LIVE IN?

How important to you are modern conveniences like indoor plumbing?

QUITE ←

→ NOT

Post-1950 loops *Jacob*
Majority are American. Talk to ~~Abraham Portman~~ for dissuasive warnings about American loops.

Pre-1950 loops
Would friends describe you as "outdoorsy"?

NOT PARTICULARLY

YES, I LOVE THE OUTDOORS

Are you bothered by squalor and noise?

← YES

NO

Miss Barbet's loop, Austrian Alps, 1790

AND I CAN YODEL

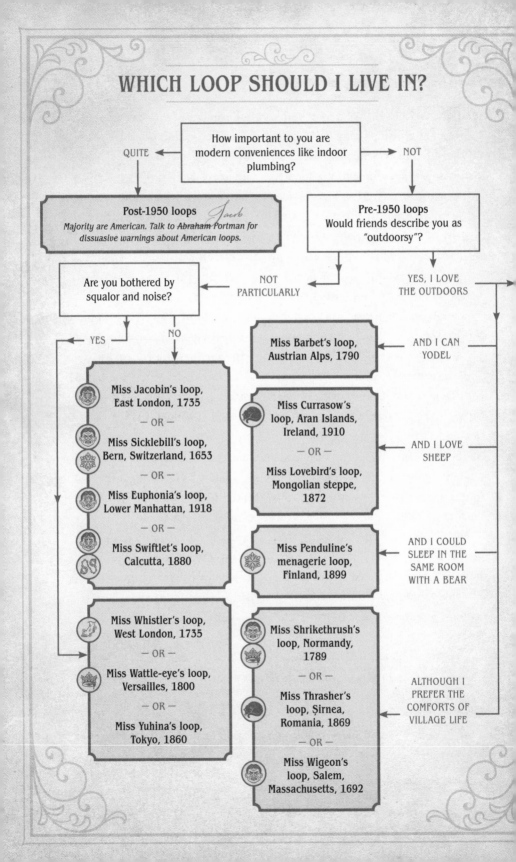

Miss Jacobin's loop, East London, 1735

— OR —

Miss Sicklebill's loop, Bern, Switzerland, 1653

— OR —

Miss Euphonia's loop, Lower Manhattan, 1918

— OR —

Miss Swiftlet's loop, Calcutta, 1880

Miss Currasow's loop, Aran Islands, Ireland, 1910

— OR —

Miss Lovebird's loop, Mongolian steppe, 1872

AND I LOVE SHEEP

Miss Penduline's menagerie loop, Finland, 1899

AND I COULD SLEEP IN THE SAME ROOM WITH A BEAR

Miss Whistler's loop, West London, 1735

— OR —

Miss Wattle-eye's loop, Versailles, 1800

— OR —

Miss Yuhina's loop, Tokyo, 1860

Miss Shrikethrush's loop, Normandy, 1789

— OR —

Miss Thrasher's loop, Şirnea, Romania, 1869

— OR —

Miss Wigeon's loop, Salem, Massachusetts, 1692

ALTHOUGH I PREFER THE COMFORTS OF VILLAGE LIFE

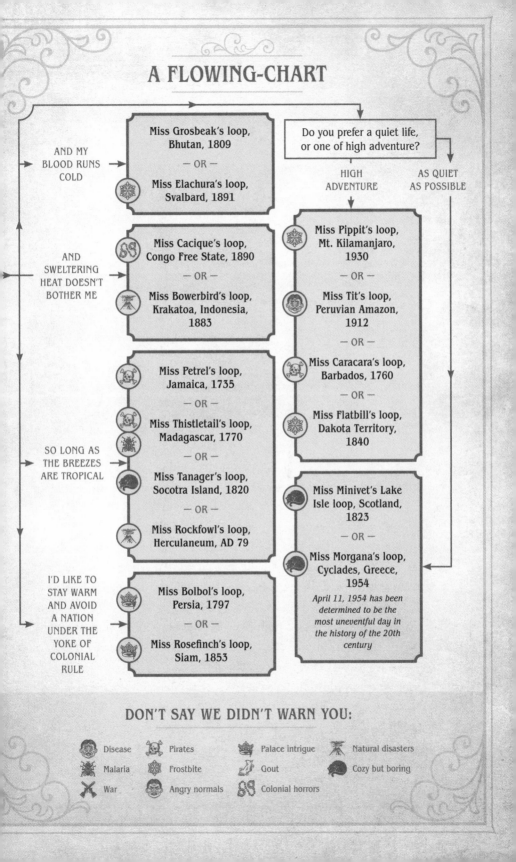

FOCUS ON:
Florida

Tampa Bay's resident cryptid, a sea lizard named Spencer.

Florida has been a refuge for the strange, the hunted, and the unwanted for as long as anyone can remember. Its baffling geography is rife with hiding places: vast swamps, mangrove forests, ever-shifting rivers of grass, and an unmappable proliferation of tiny islands. It was also the winter home to many of the circuses and carnivals that toured America throughout the twentieth century, and thus became a permanent refuge for legions of retired clowns, animal trainers, and sideshow performers. The town of Gibsonton was at one point populated almost entirely by sideshow folk, with many peculiars among them. The fire chief stood over nine feet tall, the sheriff was a sword-swallower who dined on carpet nails, and special zoning laws allowed residents to keep elephants and giraffes in their gardens. Eventually the town became rather *too* well-known, an attraction unto itself, and as sightseers came to gawk, the peculiars who lived there drifted away to lesser-known parts of the state.

····→ THE DANGERS OF TIME LOOPS ←····

Time loops have preserved our lives for millennia. If we have thrived as a people, even minorly, or been able to gather in numbers and form societies and systems of government, we have time loops to thank for it. For many of us they have become a womb of safety and comfort. But there is a dark side to our dependency on loops, a danger that becomes clear and present when we are forced to leave them. It's a pair of dangers, really: First, that many peculiars have lived apart from present-day normals for so long that when we reenter society we're like innocents abroad, strangers in our own country, and easy targets for hoodlums, bamboozlers, and wights. Of course, there are certainly peculiars who are savvy in the ways of normals and can move quite effortlessly through the present. But the second danger threatens even these smooth operators, for it is a universal threat to all who've lived in loops: rapid aging. There are so many ways to come to grief as a result of rapid aging that I cannot hope to discuss them all here. I pray it will be sufficient to enumerate the most common mishaps and lay out some prophylactic measures which may prevent you too, Dear Reader, from coming to grief.

There is an old Latin motto commonly found upon both gravestones and the lintels of doorways to ymbrynes' homes: Tempus edax rerum. "Time is the devourer of all things." That cheery old chestnut was so popular in my girlhood that it was adapted into a song sung at birthday parties and a lullaby cooed into the cribs of young children. Thankfully, it is no longer in vogue, yet the point, if not the music, is worth remembering. We cannot cheat time.

Loops do not make peculiars immortal, despite the fact that we don't age while inside them. Skipped time is banked away, creating a tower of temporal debt that comes crashing down if one spends too long outside a loop. Generally speaking, a time-indebted peculiar can exist outside their loop for a day without consequence. Many peculiars, especially younger ones, can go up to three days without aging forward, but never longer. The rule of thumb is to limit out-of-loop sojourns to less than twenty-four hours.

Once the traveling peculiar returns to a loop, they should stay inside it for at least as many hours as they were in the present. If they hurry out again without allowing sufficient recovery time, they risk aging forward even more quickly. Should they overstay their limit in the present, the penalty is fast and harsh. It can take a few hours for the skipped time to return, their body experiencing a gradual withering like fruit left to dry in the sun, or it can come upon them all in a rush, their hair graying and bones hollowing in a few minutes. If the debt is only weeks or months—even a small number of years—the result may be disorienting, but not overly injurious. Rapid aging of ten years or more is liable to damage the brain. Anything greater than fifty tends to render the poor subject skeletal. I once witnessed a man named Flimsburgh age one hundred and twelve years in three minutes as his reward for an overindulgent weekend spent frolicking in the present (and a missed alarm clock).

The unfortunate Flimsburgh.

The simplest way to avoid such a fate is to heed closely the number of hours spent outside your loop, and to always assume you have less time than you think to make it back to safety. Any number of things may conspire to waylay you, such as harassment by police—many have aged forward in a present-day jail cell after having been too flagrantly peculiar in the presence of normals, then been released by the confused jailer, who returns to check on his young prisoner only to discover an old person in their place (or a pile of bones). I suppose it's naive to think that peculiar children could possibly resist displaying their abilities in front of normals, and yet resist it you must, Reader. We ymbrynes have better things to do than search every jail and orphanage whenever one of you fails to return from some errand.

Another way peculiars fall victim to rapid aging: They become lost while traveling in the present and fail to find a loop entrance quickly enough. Loop entrances are, for obvious reasons, hidden, and with rare exceptions, we don't print maps of them.[5] When journeying between one loop and another, peculiars are expected to commit the directions to memory; we cannot take the chance of written directions falling into the wrong hands. Clues written in sufficiently complex code are permitted, as are normal maps with very wide areas circled—enough to jog the memory of a peculiar who's been told where a certain loop entrance is, but so general that the information would be of little use to an enemy. (Even if some malefactor discovered that a particular loop entrance was within a ten-block radius of a certain section of London, how on earth would they go about finding it, when a loop entrance can be as small as a cubbyhole?)

But memories falter, and some loop entrances are so well hidden that even peculiars who've been told exactly where to find them sometimes fail to do so. The consequences are tragic, as many a desiccated corpse discovered only a short distance from a loop entrance can attest. So, before embarking on a journey between loops, first consult your ymbryne. If she grants you permission to leave, she may choose to accompany you. If that isn't possible, she will furnish you with directions to be memorized, and perhaps a travel partner, for there is safety in numbers.

Emergencies do arise, however, and circumstances may force you to flee your loop without consulting an ymbryne. You may not know the precise location of the loop you are seeking. You may have only rough directions, or none at all. In such cases it is essential that you have a general understanding of how to locate hidden loop entrances, so you might at least make an educated guess, and avoid the fate of poor Mr. Flimsburgh.

---

5. One exception is the *Map of Days*, copies of which are exceedingly rare and closely guarded. The Americans, who make a distinction between public and private loops, have printed maps of the public ones, some of which function like temporal hotels for the weary peculiar traveler. We can only assume they made some unsavory deal with the wights—I shudder to think what the terms might have been—which convinced the wights not to destroy these loops or use them as convenient feeding troughs for their hollowgast. Regardless, we in Europe came to no such understanding, and so peculiars who are traveling from loop to loop rarely have the benefit of carrying a printed map with them.

·····→ HIDDEN LOOP ENTRANCES ←·····
AND HOW TO FIND THEM

S o, how does one go about finding a hidden loop entrance? There are various techniques you might employ, depending on the situation. What follows are the most reliable methods.

SEEK YE THE SHADOWS

It's best if we're not seen entering and exiting loops, so ymbrynes tend to keep their entrances well hidden from public view. If you suspect a loop entrance to be in a particular house, check the tucked-away parts first: the attic, the cellar, the coal bin, the dungeon. Long, dark passageways are a favorite, so make sure to scout nearby tunnels, subterranean passageways, sewers, underground train platforms, and the undersides of bridges. Note, too, that the passageway does not have to be oriented horizontally: Wide-mouthed chimneys and water wells have also been used as loop entrances. If you're going to go poking around the chimneys and cellars of old houses, consider posing as a county inspector. A clipboard, hard hat, and high-visibility vest will gain you entrance to all manner of otherwise private places.

When searching for loop entrances inside a castle (where they are fairly common), check the edges of hanging portraits for hinges that might swing away to reveal a passage. Inquire after any subterranean chambers. Look

Dark tunnels and passageways are good places to hunt for loop entrances.

for brickwork, wallpaper, or wood paneling that doesn't match the age of the house, for this can be a sign that an old door has been covered over. Train your eye to search for hidden seams in floors and walls. If you can obtain schematic drawings of the building, look for unusually thick dead spaces between walls. These may contain secret passages.

In the main, castles are more likely to contain loop entrances than old houses, as castles are con-

The hasty escape of a peculiar gentleman.

sidered more permanent and less likely to be demolished. Ymbrynes do not like having the buildings that contain their loop entrances knocked down; imagine an entrance that had been on the third floor of a house but now is naked to the world and suspended thirty feet in the air. Most inconvenient.

A CERTAIN TINGLE IN THE SPINE

Now and then a curious creeping sensation can be felt when one nears a loop entrance. This could manifest as a tingle along the spine, a raising of the fine hairs on one's neck, or even a sudden need to use the privy. Stay alert for these subtle changes.

WAIT AND WATCH

If you have the time to spare and are in no imminent danger of rapid aging, one tried-and-true technique is to post oneself in the vicinity of a suspected loop and stake it out. Wait long enough, and you're likely to see another peculiar pass by. You need only follow them.

HAUNT THE HAUNTED PLACES

Familiarize yourself with local lore. Seek out places that have a reputation for being haunted, as scare stories about monsters, ghouls, and avenging spirits are often a pretext invented to keep the normal population at bay (or are the result of real encounters with peculiars, who are sometimes assumed to be supernatural). The locals most familiar with these tales are usually teenagers, though interviewing them without raising their suspicions can be a challenge.

Loop entrance (eighth tomb from right, middle row), Crypt of the Zouaves, Rome.

Relatedly, graveyards are a common site for loop entrances, as are crypts, funeral homes, charnel houses, and potter's fields.

CROSS YE THE WATER

Ymbrynes love islands, and for good reason: They are isolated, easily defensible, fully controllable spaces upon which to establish a loop. (I myself chose an island for my loop—one that had hosted many loops before it—and though it meant my wards rarely got the chance to sample city life, I believe they were none the worse for the deprivation.) Look for islands not just off coastlines, but within the bounds of cities, too. You may be surprised at the number of small islands that are hidden in urban areas, and the loops that are concealed upon them: North Brother, Hart, and Roosevelt Islands in New York City; Poveglia Island in the Venice Lagoon; Eel Pie Island on London's River Thames, among other examples. To reach them, consider hiring a small boat and a discreet (read: bribable) captain.

····→ SOME EXAMPLES OF ←····
UNUSUAL LOOP ENTRANCES

I present these here both to demonstrate the endless ingenuity of ymbrynes and because many loop entrances bear a familial resemblance to one another. Studying these may help you puzzle out the location of a loop in the future.

THE VANISHING ISLAND OF INCHMAHOME, STIRLINGSHIRE, SCOTLAND

There is a loop entrance in the drowned ruins of an old stone church on the tidal island of Inchmahome, which vanishes beneath the foggy Lake of Menteith for all but a few minutes in the early morning of every third day, when it can be accessed by boat. The entrance is in a trapdoor in the transept of the roofless church, which even at low tide will be partially flooded, so wear a good pair of rubbers, bring a hooked pole to open the trap and fend off the lake's giant freshwater octopus, and for heaven's sake, don't dally.

HERMIT'S HOUSEBOAT ON A DRY LAKE, IMPERIAL DESERT, CALIFORNIA

The lake is dry in the present day but not in the century-old loop, so prepare for a bit of sailing to reach your destination after crossing over. Miss Bustard is the ymbryne here, and her settlement is clearly visible on the lake's western shore. If you have trouble piloting the boat, fire off one of the flares stored beside the life vests and someone will row out to retrieve you.

THE MIDPOINT OF A RAILROAD BRIDGE, YUKON TERRITORY

I strongly recommend consulting the train schedule before attempting to enter this loop. There have been . . . mishaps.

"LEAP OF FAITH" TOWER, FAR NORTH QUEENSLAND, AUSTRALIA

This curious loop entrance can only be accessed by a body traveling at a velocity of at least 9.8 meters per second. The simplest way to achieve this is by leaping off this purpose-built tower at a spot marked by an X. A normal jumper will fall to his death; a peculiar one will cross into Miss Frogmouth's loop, where a giant haystack will break their fall.

S-MART SUPERSTORE, FREEZER AISLE, BIRMINGHAM, ENGLAND

This is an example of an old loop built in an old structure—in this case a manor house dating from the sixteenth century—which was inherited by a new structure when the manor house was torn down and a modern shopping center built in its place. The loop entrance, formerly hidden behind a panel of wainscoting in the manor's considerable library, is now located behind the ice creams in the freezer aisle of this store—the racks swing out of the way to admit entrance. Borrow a blue employee smock from the break room to attract minimal attention.

MAX-IVOR MOTEL, ROOM 308, OUTSIDE LINCOLN, NEBRASKA

Some loops have been created in places that are convenient to the peculiar traveler. In the United States, they often parallel major highways and are spaced a few hundred miles apart in order to provide regular places to stop, rest, take a meal with fellow peculiars, and prevent rapid aging.

DOUBLE H OIL PIPELINE, TEXHOMA, TEXAS

A very unusual loop entrance. Miss Bronzewing (pictured, in furs) is the only ymbryne ever to establish a loop entrance inside an oil pipeline (that I am aware of). Once a week, at a time known only to Miss Bronzewing, the pipeline goes briefly dry. This is the only time the loop can be accessed, via a subtle door in a certain section of conduit.

····→ A NOTE ABOUT ←····
BOOBY-TRAPPED LOOP ENTRANCES

Occasionally, there have been cases of loops—generally ones that are in special danger of discovery by wights—that have had their entrances rigged with death traps. To enter them you must not only know the location of the entrance but also have received

Miss Bronzewing atop her oil pipeline loop entrance.

The death trap.

instructions on the method of bypassing the trap. Here is one example, of a now-collapsed loop in an old ruined Tudor house in Lincolnshire, England:

In the stateroom of Skellingthorpe Manor is the family shield that, when one part is touched, revolves, and a flight of steps becomes visible. The first, second, and fourth steps are to be trusted, but to tread any of the others is to set in motion concealed machinery that causes the staircase to collapse, disclosing a vault some seventy feet in depth, down which the unwary are precipitated.

·····➔ TOURIST LOOPS ◆·····

L argely a thing of the past, tourist loops are a relic of an era before wights and hollowgast forced us to hide inside our loops like fugitives. During that more peaceful time, in the rare interbellum periods when there were no continent-spanning wars between normals, it was common for ymbrynes to take their wards on trips to other times. This predated the Panloopticon, so in order to see Venice in its sixteenth-century heyday, for instance, one did actually have to travel to La Serenissima by train or boat. The loop entrance was on the nearby quarantine island of Poveglia, and it spanned the entire Venetian lagoon in the summer of 1570. Tourist loops were highly *en vogue* throughout the latter half of the nineteenth century, right up to the creation of the hollowgast in 1908. They required a great deal of labor to operate: several ymbrynes to reset the largest loops; costumers to dress visitors in period-accurate clothes; guides and chaperones to steer them clear of trouble; and in certain loops, a small cadre of bodyguards to deal with potentially dangerous looped normals (thugs, highwaymen, or those so disturbed by our presence that they became violent). Tragically, most of our tourist loops were easy targets for the hollowgast. The few that remain are now fiercely protected, and considered treasures of peculiardom.

A SHORT EXCERPT FROM

Peculiar Travels on Land and Sea

a once-popular guide-book, now sadly out of print,
which elucidates some of the delights and
challenges of loop tourism.

VENICE
CARNIVAL SEASON OF 1570

The Grand Canal.

A bustling, multicultural place where the peculiar is sure to feel at home and will rarely be stared at. There's so much to see in its palaces, squares, and markets that at the end of a day of touring, one's eyes ache from looking. Then as now, highlights include St. Mark's Square, the Rialto market, and the Grand Canal. Carnival with its elaborate masked balls is a particular time in Venice where peculiars mingle with ease.

The Venice loop's entrance, in the vine-choked ruins of an old asylum on the forsaken quarantine island of Poveglia, is just a short vaporetto ride from Piazza San Marco. A hundred thousand were stuffed into mass graves here during plague times, and rumors that the island is packed to the gunwales with ghosts have kept most normals at bay, the occasional thrill seeker notwithstanding. Beware the hidden pit of spikes and the occasional camera-toting "urban explorer."

Dressed for a Venetian masked ball.

Venice's loop entrance, in the old asylum.

Shop 'til you drop in old Shanghai.

SHANGHAI

A NICE DAY IN THE FALL OF 1867

A favorite with collectors of fine pottery and precious objects, this Shanghai loop deposits you into the heart of a bustling market.

MACHU PICCHU

SUMMER SOLSTICE, 1450

Intrepid Miss Pilotbird has kept this loop humming along for over five hundred years. Despite the obvious challenges involved in reaching the site, visitors say it's more than worth the journey. The locals are friendly, the views breathtaking. If you make the trek to see her, be a dear and bring Miss Pilotbird a sack of candy bars; she loves them.

BLOODY GULCH MINING CAMP
SIERRA NEVADA MOUNTAINS, CALIFORNIA, 1849
(ADULTS ONLY PLEASE)

Temporal travelers have long been fascinated with the American West during its so-called frontier period (though it was only a "frontier" to usurping newcomers of European descent; others had already lived there for thousands of years). Perhaps the pulp-fiction dime novels our youth are so fond of have romanticized this bloody period beyond all believability, making it seem like some sort of rough-and-tumble playground where a "tenderfoot" can go to "prove his grit" or "earn her spurs" by tossing lassos about and using herds of perfectly innocent buffalo for rifle practice. There is also a pernicious myth that despite a few gunslinging "bad apples," places like the Bloody Gulch mining camp are filled with essentially kind souls who are positively bursting with good, clean "pioneer spirit." In truth, there are many more bad apples than good, and by "bad" I mean murderous psychopaths, hopeless drunks, heartless opportunists, and all manner of shady characters.

But attempts to discourage visits here have so far been unsuccessful, so rather than leave the Bloody Gulch tourist loop a tantalizing mystery, which

Accommodations in Bloody Gulch are subpar.

Miss Rebecca Greylag, proprietor.

is apt to attract even more visitors, we will arm you with a few warnings: Trust no one; travel here only in groups of three or more; avoid the gambling halls; and heed Miss Greylag, the salty ymbryne who maintains this loop. The only accommodations are at a flea-infested shack that the locals optimistically call a hotel, where price gouging is common practice, and eye gouging more common still. The local entertainments are drinking, gaming, and carousing, all of which are strictly forbidden to peculiars traveling abroad. Permitted activities include viewing a train robbery, learning about the ill effects of syphilis, rescuing a party of stranded travelers who are mere hours from resorting to cannibalism (hiking shoes required), and descending into a gold mine with Miss Greylag.

SHOULD YOU REQUIRE MEDICAL ATTENTION WHILE TRAVELING

Beware local doctors, and if possible wait until returning to your home loop to seek attention. We recommend bringing a first-aid kit with you, and larger groups should always travel with a bone-mender.

Local "sawbones,"
Bloody Gulch, Calif.

····➔ TOURIST LOOPS ◆···· OF RECENT VINTAGE

PAMPLONA, SPAIN

THE RUNNING OF THE BULLS, 1928

This cretinous loop was all the rage with a certain macho contingent of peculiar tourist for quite a number of years. It was maintained by the same ghastly fiends who operated the Devil's Acre blood-sport arena, and

despite multiple bans and concerted attempts by the Ymbryne Council to shut it down, illicit entrances kept cropping up like pustules on a plague sufferer. Attendees claimed they were training to outrun hollowgast, but it seemed to me they were more interested in bragging rights. Miss Wren ran a sting against the loop's organizers in the 1950s, and once they'd been rounded up, she forced them to sprint down a long alley lined with animals all braying and slapping at them. After photographs of their humiliation were published in the *Muckraker,* they slunk away to distant loops in America and were not heard from again.

THE "BEST MOTEL BREAKFAST IN AMERICA"

CONNECTICUT, 1963

Hartford's humble Imbre Inn serves soggy eggs, stale cereal, rubbery bacon, and a rare juice that supposedly enhances peculiar ability.

It's that good.

THE COMPLAINTS OF A PECULIAR TRAVELER REGARDING THE STATE OF EUROPEAN INNS DURING THE SEVENTEENTH CENTURY

EXCERPTED FROM AN ACCOUNT BY CHARLES OGIER,

TRANSLATED FROM THE LATIN BY E. S. BATES

It is a most unsatisfactory thing, merely reading about places you would like to see in person; but if seeing seventeenth-century Europe means sleeping in seventeenth-century inns, there is much to be said for preferring the experience in print only.

Expecting Italian innkeepers to provide clean sheets is expecting too much, and as the nation is grievously afflicted with the itch, it is desirable for the visitor to carry his own bedding. In many cases, too, we find the tourist sleeping on a table in his clothes to avoid the dirtiness of the bed, or the vermin. Still, in Spain, you share your bed with these permanent occupants only—a result of the enforcement of the penalty of burning alive for canoodling. In Germany, the custom is just the reverse; in fact, if the tourist does not find a companion for himself, the host will choose one for him, and his bedfellow might be a gentleman, or he might be a laborer; all that can safely be prophesied about him is that he will be drunk when he comes to bed. In Germany, as many beds are stuffed in a room as the room will hold. In Saxony, there are no beds, no benches, no fire, even. All lie in the straw among the cows, the chief disadvantage of which is that your pillow is liable to be eaten in the night.

Protection from unscrupulous hosts is rare. A stricter system might have been a check on the murdering innkeeper, to whom I have heard occasional references; one had been detected at Poitiers shortly before the arrival of a friend of mine, and at Stralsund, another tale runs, eight hundred (!) persons had disappeared at one inn. They had reappeared—it is true—pickled.

····→ TOURISM AND THE PERILS ←····
OF LEAPFROGGING

For peculiar tourists, the ancient world holds innumerable attractions: opportunities to view history's greatest art and architecture when they were new; to hold discussions with philosophers whose ideas still shape our thinking today; to participate in lively pagan festivals; to brush up on ancient Greek, Latin, or Persian with native speakers. Sadly, no loops from that era survive.[6] There were not many to begin with, as the ancients were relatively enlightened on the matter of peculiarness and rarely persecuted us so long as we didn't disrupt the order of their empires. As a result, the ancient world can only be reached by leapfrogging backward through dozens of collapsed loops, a journey so complicated and dangerous it's considered practically impossible by temporal travel agents.

The most straightforward route requires visiting no fewer than twenty-one loops and tracking endlessly back and forth across Europe and Asia Minor, the world growing more barbaric with each leap backward in time. Soon you predate the few passable roads built during the Renaissance; the cities shrink and are subsumed by trackless forests teeming with wolves; and the people you meet are as likely to kill you as ask your name. The chief problem is the Dark Ages, stretching like a vast desert of twelve hundred years between the fall of Rome and the Renaissance. A frightful lack of infrastructure is one difficulty: The Huns, Visigoths, and Saxons who sacked Rome in the fifth century did nothing to maintain the empire's roads, bridges, harbors, stone buildings, and flood control systems, and they hadn't the first idea how to replace them once they fell apart. (It speaks volumes that in the year 1500, after ten centuries of neglect, the Romans' highways were still the best in Europe.) The same journey of thirty miles, comfortably done in half a day in the eighteenth century, is a nightmarish, days-long slog through bandit-infested forests in the ninth century—or, heaven forefend, the seventh.

---

6. None that we know about, anyway.

Permit me the indulgence of boldface type to impart this next bit of advice: **If you value your life even a little, avoid seventh-century Europe at all costs.** It is the worst, most appalling, most bloodthirsty, most light-less reach of the Dark Ages—though in truth it is only slightly more ap-palling than the centuries that succeeded it. It isn't the state of the roads that make it so, so much as the people. The Dark Ages mind is alien territory: Their deep ignorance, paranoia, and superstition are stagger-ing, as is their comfort with extreme and sudden violence. It's strange to consider, but people today have more in common with those who lived two thousand years ago than with those just eight hundred years gone. Consider that most people in the Dark Ages lived all their lives in tiny, inbred hamlets, and rarely left them. A journey to a village twenty miles distant was akin to visiting another country, and the dialect spoken from one to the next could be incomprehensibly different. If one was cast to the wind by war or some natural disaster, a return home was practically impossible. There were no maps, few roads, and insufficient markings on what roads there were, though most villages were nameless anyway. Many people had no names themselves, other than some undignified sobriquet—Goatherd, Redhead, One-Leg, One-Leg's Daughter. There was no writing; even kings were illiterate. They had no clocks, no calen-dars, no concept of time at all other than the changing seasons. Few had any idea even what century they were living in.

Perhaps I belabor the point. This is all to illustrate that the sudden intrusion of a stranger, especially one whose clothes are more than rags and skins and whose language is different or oddly accented, would be as baffling and alarming to them as an invasion by space aliens. The natural reaction would simply be to kill you with whatever blunt object is closest to hand. More thoughtful Dark Agers may instead accuse you of being a witch or the devil in disguise and subject you to unsurvivable ordeals in order to determine your innocence, be it drowning, burning, or fall-ing from a great height. Survivors are evidently guilty, and they will only redouble their efforts to kill you.

So, please. As tempting as a genuine Roman Bacchanalia might sound, it isn't worth the trip.

····➔ A BRIEF NOTE ON ◆····
PUBLIC EXECUTIONS

Unhappily, these macabre spectacles are difficult for the historical traveler to avoid. Hangings, beheadings, burnings, drownings, stonings, wheel-breakings, gibbetings, and other diverse forms of capital punishment were applied liberally and nearly always in public, often preceded by mutilations. Apart from fairs and feast days, they were the most common form of mass entertainment throughout Europe over the preceding two millennia. I urge those of fragile constitution to avoid public squares altogether during daytime hours. Also, however much your conscience rebels against this barbarism, I implore you not to intercede—crowds of bloodthirsty peasants do not look kindly upon having their amusements interrupted and would happily string you up next to the condemned fellow, should they manage to get their unwashed hands on you. And, as you surely know by now, tempus edax rerum. The wretch you save today will still have been separated from his head tomorrow, despite your best efforts.

Fun in the sun, fifteenth-century style.

·····➔ PUNISHMENT LOOPS ◆·····

In an ideal world, punishment loops would be unnecessary. Then again, in such a world, peculiars would be fully accepted members of society, and time loops would never have been necessary at all. Alas, the world is a garden filled with snakes, and peculiars are but human, capable of the same failings and frailties to which normalkind is prone. We are not exempt from greed, envy, malice, nor any of the other, darker impulses of the heart. You may read more about this in the chapter on some of our criminal peculiars (where you'll find a list of our more infamous inmates), but for our purposes here, suffice it to say that on occasion, blessedly rare though they may be, peculiars commit crimes of such magnitude that they must be isolated from their fellows.

Exile from peculiar society has sometimes been used as a punishment, though in the case of our most odious malefactors, this is viewed as akin to dumping a load of particularly noxious trash in a neighbor's yard; it isn't fair to the normals. There, too, the criminal is likely to run amok, upsetting normals, drawing unneeded attention to peculiarkind, and likely causing as much trouble for us *outside* peculiar society as they did while they were in it. Unless a truly remote exile can be found—Arctic islands are preferred—then purpose-built punishment loops are often the best solution.

Punishment loops are not jails in the usual sense. You won't find cells or bars or chains, except in the cases of the very worst offenders. Dungeons and oubliettes are inhumane, and anyway, such jails cannot hold us: We have innumerable methods of picking locks, slipping through bars, enchanting the minds of jailers, etc. We've learned it's better to imprison our criminals in small, easily controlled, closed loops (closed, in that they have no exit to the outer past). The number of prisoners in each is kept low to make organized uprisings unlikely. Jail terms are long; fifty years is the average sentence. Most peculiars are so accustomed to living in loops that the passage of time has become relative, and a year can elapse almost without one noticing. Shorter sentences are simply not much of a deterrent.

The loops are, as a rule, unpleasant. Who would object to spending a century in paradise? Devil's Acre is the best known, but when the wights made it their stronghold it ceased being a punishment loop.

What follows is a sampling of both well-known and obscure punishment loops.

LOCHRANZA CASTLE, SCOTLAND, DURING an ENGLISH SIEGE, AD 923

This is a most unpleasant loop. The siege is in its second month, and the castle's besieged inhabitants are starved, traumatized, demoralized, and diseased. There is little to eat that isn't infested with rats and weevils, the weather is damp and bitterly cold, the castle's firewood long since consumed, and the English catapult dead livestock over the castle walls all day long. The only entertainment to be had is in figuring out, day after looped day, how to sneak out of the castle and slip in amongst the invaders without being skewered on their lances, for the English army is well stocked with food and ale, and I have heard that, during breaks between their flaming arrow barrages and corpse catapultings, they have a very good time indeed.

Alexander
Dubois
Zvonimir von
Lothringen.

MOST INFAMOUS (AND LONGEST-SERVING) RESIDENT: Alexander Dubois
Zvonimir von Lothringen

CRIME: Malicious interference in normal affairs. He murdered several
royals in the Low Countries and Saxony during the eighteenth century in
order to push them into war with one another—for no reason other than
his own sadistic entertainment. It's the sort of behavior we might expect
from wights, but will never tolerate among our own people.

TERM OF SENTENCE: Five hundred years

The Steamship *Chunder.*

THE STEAMSHIP *CHUNDER* DURING a STORMY CROSSING OF THE IRISH CHANNEL, 1935

One of the few nautical loops in existence, the *Chunder* plies a Sisyphean route between Ireland and Wales during one of the most stomach-churning storms of the 1930s. At times the deck tilts to nearly ninety degrees, and when the unhappy passengers aren't heaving up their lunch, they're lashing themselves to the mast to keep from being pitched into the freezing water. Forward motion is nearly impossible; the boat is entirely at the mercy of the sea. A passage that would take only a few hours under normal circumstances is lengthened to nearly twenty-four, and just as the storm abates and the longed-for harbor comes distantly into view, the loop resets and the whole awful journey has to be endured again. And again. And again.

Miranda Lindworth.

MOST INFAMOUS RESIDENT: Miranda Lindworth

CRIMES: Impersonating an ymbryne; entrapment of twelve unsuspecting innocents; trafficking said children to the wights

TERM OF SENTENCE: Ninety-nine years and a day (one day added for referring to Miss Avocet as a "mutton shunter")

ELKHART, KANSAS, "BLACK SUNDAY," 1935

A cloud of dust ten thousand feet high turns this town "black as three midnights in a box," according to a traumatized resident who survived it. Birds and rabbits flee the leading edge in terror, but there is nowhere for the humans of Elkhart to retreat but to their flimsy houses, into which the dust seeps relentlessly. This storm—the worst of the whole bleak Dust Bowl era—carried more dirt in it than was excavated from the Panama Canal in seven years of digging. Standing outside in the wind is like having one's flesh abraded with steel wool. Huddling indoors during the worst of it isn't much better. Prisoners here must wear dust masks and goggles at all hours and are advised to keep their nostrils lubricated with lamp oil. There is grit and dust in everything: in the air, in one's hair, in every bite of food. Every tree and garden has been stripped bare by previous "dusters." The highlight of Black Sunday is the funeral wake of Mrs. Ida Haggerty, which proceeds for only twenty minutes before the scouring wind rises up to scatter the mourners and their repast.

Try the lemon cake.

MOST INFAMOUS RESIDENT: Rusty "The Cannibal" Gearheart

CRIME: Nonpayment of library fines; cannibalism

TERM OF SENTENCE: Seventy-five years

HOW *to* CONDUCT ONESELF *in the* PRESENT

As I write this, we have recently embarked into the twenty-first century. Thanks to the emergence of hollowgast in 1908, most of us have been confined to loops for nearly one hundred years; some even longer. The world outside was once familiar. It was the place of our birth and coming-of-age; its physical geography is in many ways unchanged. And yet, almost without our noticing, it has become a foreign country, its people alien to us. We have only to walk through the exit of our temporal home, a distance of perhaps a few hundred meters, to become strangers in a strange land. And it is a land filled with dangers.

It cannot be avoided. You may need to cross through the present to reach another loop. You may be asked by your ymbryne to purchase some necessary thing that is only available in the modern present (medicine, for instance, or liquid fabric softener). Or you may simply be curious about what's "out there." Whatever the reason, the moment you set foot outside your loop, your ability to adapt and blend will be tested, and failures can be every bit as deadly as rapid aging. The modus operandi of every out-of-loop peculiar should be to avoid attracting unwanted attention. We must blend in as best we can, and attempt to "pass" as normal for as long as we are in normal company. Though it can be exhausting to hide your true nature for hours or days at a stretch, and though you'll be tempted to let your peculiarity show itself just as surely as someone with a bad itch is tempted to scratch, you must never let down your guard.

Assume someone is always peeping at you through the hedges or listening at the door. That the man who appears to be sleeping in the train car beside you is faking it—and there is a camera in the bridge of his glasses and a microphone in his bow tie. Our enemies are perpetually searching for us (more on them in the chapter on wights), and they are much better at posing as normal than we are. Also troublesome is the tendency for some normals to find us unaccountably fascinating, even when we are perfectly camouflaged and our modern-day accents and lingo are polished. Some normals are drawn to us for reasons they don't comprehend and will find themselves staring at us, straining to overhear us, even following us. If they are allowed to witness something peculiar, their fascination becomes an obsession that can only be broken by a memory-wipe, and sometimes not even then. In a worst-case scenario, this can be just as dangerous as an enemy who consciously means us harm. (For more on how normals can prove so dangerous—even sweet-seeming ones who aren't wielding pitchforks or kindling a bonfire—please refer to "The Dangers of Exposure.")

Disguise Yourself as a Normal Person

Study how the normals in your present-day area dress, speak, and comport themselves. Styles and cultures vary from place to place and decade to decade, so I cannot provide many useful specifics here. It is your responsibility to keep abreast of normal fashions and modes of speech. One way to do this is by paying attention to their magazines, or subscribing to Miss Scrimshaw's annual digest of normal trends, *Passing Fancy*. (Just clip and drop off the subscription card at your nearest loop.)

PLEASE BEGIN MY SUBSCRIPTION TO

PASSING FANCY!

FOR FIVE YEARS ☐ £3.50   FOR FIFTY YEARS ☐ £30

NAME

ADDRESS   CITY, ETC.

POSTCODE   COUNTRY

YMBRYNE'S NAME   LOOP DATE

☐ REMITTANCE ENCLOSED   ☐ BILL ME LATER

PLEASE CONTINUE ON REVERSE ☞

····→ CHOOSE THE RIGHT COSTUME ←····

Most loops have a rack of clothing that can be borrowed from before venturing out. Choose a costume that suits your purpose in the present. You may also purchase some modestly priced clothes for yourself while in the present and keep them. Practice wearing them around your loop until you feel comfortable in them. If you feel uncomfortable, you will *appear* uncomfortable—and attract suspicion.

I recommend picking up fashion catalogs while in the present and updating your costume every ten or fifteen years, lest it fall out of style. Conserva-

A typical American costume.

tive styles are best. Avoid brightly colored or attention-getting clothes. Your objective should be for the eyes of normals to slide right past you.

- -

I AM A / AN ...

☐ YMBRYNE   ☐ INTERESTED PARTY

☐ WARD   ☐ FOLLOWER OF FASHION

☐ HABERDASHER

100% DISCOUNT FOR QUALIFYING PECULIARS

⋯⋯⟶ GENERAL ADVICE FOR ⟵⋯⋯
BLENDING INTO CROWDS

✓ Do:

Avoid eye contact.

Cover any large tattoos, scarifications, or unusual markings.

Be well-groomed without looking too stylish. Avoid hair gel or dye. If your entire face is covered in hair, consider shaving.

✗ Don't:

Forget to camouflage extra limbs. A third leg can be hidden inside roomy pants, as can most tails. A third arm can be wrapped around the neck and covered with a scarf. Extra eyes are easy to hide beneath bandages. For more information, please refer to pamphlet 502-F, *A FAREWELL TO ARMS*.

✓ Do:

Mimic the behavior of normals around you. Try choosing an average-looking normal from a crowd and mirroring them. Match their walking pace, hand gestures, facial expressions, and tone of voice until you start to feel comfortable. Should they notice you, *DO NOT* kill them.

✗ Do not:

Follow them home, wait until they are sleeping, sneak into their house, and try on their clothes in the soft, quiet dark.

✗ And especially do not:

Forget who you are. Some peculiars are so adept at passing as normal that they come to prefer living in the present. But comfort breeds complacency, and these peculiars are much more likely to be discovered, age forward, be snatched by wights, or otherwise wind up in trouble.

"An octopus in a tuxedo is still an octopus."

—PECULIAR PROVERB

Talking to Normal People

E ven the best camouflage won't help those incapable of holding basic conversations with normal people. This is where peculiars unaccustomed to the present are most vulnerable to suspicion and discovery. Conversations should be avoided when possible, kept short when unavoidable, and always be conducted with calm confidence.

····→ PRACTICE USING ←···· CONTEMPORARY LINGO

Don't overuse modern slang. Like truffle salt in cod broth, just a pinch will do. And be very certain about the era of your lingo; employing an outdated idiom is worse than using none at all. (A phrase like "Horsefeathers, she's a choice bit of calico!" might've earned you a knowing wink in 1930, but will only confuse people nowadays.) Refer to our somewhat recent publication on the subject: *Say What? 500 Far-Out Phrases to Help You Sound Normal Right Now* (new edition for 1973).

····➔ INVENT A "NORMAL" IDENTITY ✦····

In the course of conversation you may be asked basic questions about yourself, and to avoid saying something strange or being caught in a lie, you should be prepared with answers. I recommend contriving a false identity: a new, common-sounding name; a birthday that roughly matches your apparent physical age; and a believable but unremarkable biography that won't invite further questions. If you appear to be under the age of eighteen, you may need to explain where your parents are or what you're doing out of school. Telling normals you've just gone out to buy a pint of milk will usually suffice for an answer. Having an ID card with your false name printed on it can also be useful. These can be obtained at novelty shops in urban areas or from leery-looking fellows at university fraternity parties.

····➔ TECHNIQUES FOR ✦····
ENDING CONVERSATIONS QUICKLY

The following approaches have proven effective:

➤ Ask the normal to help you move some furniture, drive you to a distant airport, or buy a magazine subscription.

➤ Uncontrollable coughing.

➤ "Suddenly realize" you are late for a pressing engagement (train, job, funeral).

➤ If all else fails, drop a Reeking Miasma tablet on the floor and grind it underfoot. Your interlocutor will quickly depart.

May I Make Friends *with* Normals?

Edward G. of Gambier, Ohio, writes:

Dear Miss Peregrine,
I don't get along with the other wards in my loop. Our loop entrance is on a college campus, and our ymbryne, Miss Rakefeather, has encouraged us to audit classes there. The normal students are quite friendly and have extended me several invitations to "ragers," "keggers," "panty raids," and other social events. May I accept?

Dear Edward,

I certainly sympathize with your desire to make friends. Our lot in life can be a lonely one, especially if you don't get on, as you say, with your allotted loop-mates. The notion of turning to normals for companionship is one we have all entertained from time to time. After all, we sprang from normals and grew up with them as our parents and siblings, and if you haven't lived in your loop very long, normals may not yet seem alien to you.

But I have seen this play out many times in the past, and it invariably ends in trouble. The peculiar is careful around the normals at first, but in time they long for deeper connection. They come to believe there is one normal who is different from the others, more accepting and open-minded, who can be trusted. The peculiar may drink too much, speak too freely. A single slip of the tongue could compromise and expose them—and their ymbryne and loop-mates, too. And then the so-called friends they've

A seemingly innocent confabulation.

made will be lost anyway: The peculiar will either be forced to evacuate their loop for another one or the normals will be subjected to brain-scrambling memory-wipes and forget them.

"All men's miseries derive from
not being able to sit in a quiet room alone."

—BLAISE PASCAL

ROLE-PLAY NORMAL ENCOUNTERS
with Your Loop-Mates

Prepare for conversations with normals by practicing with friends. Invent plausible scenarios, assign yourselves roles, and have an ymbryne judge your performance. For the unimaginative, here is a sample role-play of a scenario you might encounter in the outside world.

SCENARIO: A peculiar girl encounters a businessman while waiting to cross a busy road. The girl is carrying a suitcase filled with angry wasps.

Businessman: I have a daughter about your age.

Peculiar girl: I doubt that.

Businessman: It's the middle of a weekday. Shouldn't you be in school?

Peculiar girl: I finished school forty years ago, earning a dual degree at Oxford in Automatic Writing and Radical Entomology. (*Realizes her gaffe.*) I mean, yes. I am truant from secondary school.

Businessman: Your suitcase is buzzing. Is it full of . . . bees?

Peculiar girl: Alarm clocks.

Businessman: Look, a bee just slipped out through the keyhole.

Peculiar girl: That isn't a bee, you halfwit, it's a *Polistes carnifex*, also known as an executioner wasp. (*Realizes her gaffe.*) No idea how that got in there among my alarm clocks.

(*The wasp chases the man into traffic, where he is hit by several cars.*)

Peculiar girl: Drat.

Did you catch the girl's errors?
What might the girl have done differently?

(Answer on following page)

WHATEVER YOU DO, DON'T FALL IN LOVE WITH THEM: THE SAD STORY OF GLORIA H., PECULIAR

Gloria met him at the post office where she went to retrieve her ymbryne's mail every Tuesday afternoon. Vonn was a clerk there, and he was young and handsome. At first their conversations were short and businesslike, but in time they lengthened, and when the post office was empty and there was no one else waiting in line behind Gloria, they talked of other things: the weather, the world. She found him effortlessly charming, and he seemed entranced by her.

Gloria looked forward all week to their meetings. One Tuesday afternoon, he arranged a day off work, waited for her outside the post office, and invited her to go walking with him. She gladly accepted.

Gloria began finding excuses to leave her loop and meet him on other days of the week. They were falling in love, you see. But Gloria dared not tell her ymbryne. Her romance with Vonn was strictly forbidden.

Vonn began to ask questions about her life—questions she was forbidden to answer. Still, they were infatuated with each other. Vonn told her he wanted to marry her, if she would only tell him a little about herself. Her parents, her background. He had never even seen where she lived. "Where do you go," he asked her, "and why can I only see you every other day?"

She told him half a truth and half a lie: "Because, dear, if I see you every day I will die. It would simply be too much for my heart to take."

She couldn't admit that if she saw him every day she would age into decrepitude. She couldn't tell him that she lived in a time loop or that she could turn metal into liquid with her touch. Because of her secrets, she could only give him half of herself. She would never betray her ymbryne or her loop-mates.

She said to him, "I can never tell you where I

* She should have taped the keyhole to her suitcase shut.

live, and I can never spend the night with you, and you can never ask me questions about my past. If you can accept all that, I will marry you and love you with every inch of my soul."

Vonn was so smitten that he agreed. And so they were married, in secret. They spent as much time together as they could, and the time they were forced to spend apart, which was considerable, was agony for them both. For many months, Vonn respected her wishes and did not ask her anything, though he was consumed with wondering. But one night, he begged her not to leave. "Stay with me; I want to hold you as you fall asleep. I want mine to be the first face you see in the morning. How can I truly call myself your husband if you never share my bed?"

Her heart broke. She fell asleep with him that night, then woke in a panic in the early hours of the morning; she could feel her skin beginning to wrinkle, her bones growing brittle. Slipping away while he was still sleeping, she ran to her loop as fast as she could.

She made it just in time; another minute in the present might have aged her to death. Instead she escaped with merely a webbing of crow's feet around her eyes and a thick streak of white in her rich black hair.

Unbeknownst to Gloria, Vonn had followed her that night, and camped outside her loop entrance, which was a closet in a house where no one lived. He pounded on the door, shouting her name, and stayed there until morning, baffled and frightened that something terrible had happened to his wife.

But Gloria never emerged. Miss Grebe had forbidden her from ever seeing Vonn again. She posted guards at their loop exit so that Gloria could not leave. Gloria was heartbroken.

It was a year before she was allowed to leave again—before she was finally able to convince Miss Grebe that she was no longer in love with Vonn.

It was a lie, of course. She had thought of little else but him. And the first place she went upon leaving was the post office, to find him. He was there behind the counter.

Her heart soared. She could not help herself: she ran behind the counter and threw her arms around him. But he pushed her away, a baffled look on his face.

And she realized instantly what had happened: Miss Grebe, afraid that Vonn in his heartbroken distress would alert others to the location of their loop entrance, had wiped his memory. But he had forgotten more than just the strange closet that had swallowed his wife, or the night that Gloria ran from his bed. He had forgotten her altogether. He claimed to have no memory of marrying her at all.

In fact, in the year that had elapsed since she had seen him, Vonn had married someone else.

She ran from him, weeping. She was inconsolable. She wanted to die. She nearly did, wandering the places they walked together for so long that she nearly aged to death a second time, before Miss Grebe found her and swept her back into the loop.

She hated Miss Grebe from that day hence, and never spoke a word to her ymbryne again. But she did not leave her loop. She stayed, to be near Vonn. In the years following, she haunted him like a ghost. She watched from afar as Vonn and his normal wife had children, led a life. Vonn grew old, but Gloria did not.

One day, many years later, Vonn's wife died. Gloria attended the funeral, packed with Vonn's children, grandchildren, great-grandchildren, and all their families. She did not think he would notice her—but he did. He found her after the service had ended, and his wife has been lowered into her grave. She had tried to slip away, but he stopped her. "Thank you for coming," he said. "I didn't think you would."

"But you don't remember me," she replied in surprise.

"I do," he said. "Your stepmother came to see me the night you disappeared. She told me you had nearly died—that if we stayed together it would kill you. She told me I had to let you go, and pretend not to know you. And so I did. I pretended, though it nearly killed me. I married someone else.

I tried to forget you, but I never could. I tried my whole life to stop loving you; I never could manage it."

He clasped her hand for a moment, then let his children lead him away.

They saw each other just twice more after that, to reminisce about the days when their love was young. Then Vonn grew sick and frail. Gloria attended his deathbed. She held his hand, leaned in close, and with her lips to his ear she finally told him her secrets.

"Thank you," he whispered, and his hand went slack.

He was gone. But he was smiling.

If you ask her today, Gloria will swear to anyone that it was worth the cost—a lifetime of pain for those few months of fleeting happiness. But I would not wish such a life on anyone.

Gloria   Vonn

Lore

They traded a month of happiness
for a lifetime of torment.

HOW TO HIDE IN PLAIN SIGHT WHEN YOUR PECULIARITY CANNOT BE DISGUISED . . .
And Make a Living at It

There are those of us who can easily pass for normal, and those for whom passing is close to impossible. Some of the latter type opt for a life in the shadows, fleeing from society to become hermits in forests and caves (and inspiring legends about giants, witches, fairies, and so on). Others devise brilliant methods of hiding in plain sight and spend their whole lives outside of loops without being discovered. There is much we can learn from their bravery and ingenuity. Here are a few of the ways that the undisguisably peculiar have made homes for themselves among normals over the years.

AS FORTUNE-TELLERS AND SPIRIT MEDIUMS

Some peculiars are so prodigiously gifted with clairvoyant powers that prophetic pronouncements pour forth unbidden—over breakfast, in their sleep, while passing strangers on the street—and they find it difficult, even painful, to stem the tide. Their traditional guise has been that of the psychic or fortune-teller: garishly costumed charlatans who will be ignored as frauds by most, but rewarded handsomely by a small, devoted clientele of true believers.

An Italian fortune-teller.

A spiritist and his client.

AS "CHICKEN LADIES"

The Romans were devotees of alectryomancy, a once highly respected form of divination involving the use of chickens. Grains were scattered and deep meaning attributed to the order in which they were pecked. No major decision was made without consulting a chicken, from matters of war to affairs of the heart. The *pullularii*, or "chicken ladies," entrusted with their care and grooming were, more often than not,

The Bulgarian chicken lady Ljuba Siderov, photographed in 1912, with the rooster who would later assassinate her, and his hen-wife.

99

A 1905 painting by the Russian artist Makovsky depicting alectryomancy to predict the most suitable mate for a marriageable young woman. Note the chicken lady, seated, proffering feed.

peculiar, and a few used their preternatural connections with the birds to manipulate generals and emperors, and themselves to rise to lofty heights in Roman society. Some peculiar historians have even blamed them for the empire's fall, though conflicting evidence has produced no consensus on this. Regardless, the tradition survived the empire, and alectryomancy is still practiced in some far-flung villages of Russia, Eastern Europe, and North Africa, where peculiars continue to make a respectable living as chicken ladies.

AS PATENT-MEDICINE QUACKS

Bone-menders with a peculiar talent for healing had to balance their desire to help the sick and wounded with regard for their own safety. If a serious injury was healed too quickly, cheers of "Miracle worker!" could turn to cries of "Sorcerer!" To avoid being burned alive as repayment for their services, bone-menders devised worthless "patent" medicines to credit for speedy recoveries. Strangely, the same people who would accuse them of sorcery were happy to believe that the contents of a tiny

DR. PERRY'S RENOVATOR-ELIXIR

REVERSES DEATH IN MOST PATIENTS

A legitimate bone-mender posing as a mountebank.

glass bottle could be responsible for their phenomenal recovery and were happy to pay hefty sums for the stuff.

The claims made on behalf of their medicines beggared belief, but once a gullible public was convinced of a cure's efficacy, the peculiar who administered it was free to perform real miracles without being found out. Lionel Partridge, a peculiar who posed as a quack in seventeenth-century Dublin, used to intercept patients outside the gates of the hospital. After he had gathered a sufficient number of spectators, he would deliver his pitch: "Is there any old woman amongst you troubled with the Pimple-Pamplins, whose skin is too short for her body? Try my anti-pamphastick lozenges, which discharge vertiferous cankers in superannuated maids, purgeth the brain of all cloudifying humours, and infallibly cure Dropsie, Convulsions, Chillblains, the Mange, Inconvenient Spasms, Love Melancholey, and Excessive Prattle in Elderly Persons. Be cured without sending for an illiterate surgeon, who will sooner cleanse your pockets of money than your wounds of infection!"

Others chose to specialize according to their peculiar talents. The celebrated sixteenth-century quack Thomas Botts called himself the "wyrm exterminator," and claimed that his powders and syrups had saved many lives across London. "One is a Mr. Stiles of Smithfield," he wrote in a frankly ridiculous pamphlet, "who had been dead eight and forty hours, or so thought the surgeon, who was ready to embalm the gentleman when I was summoned by his distraught widow. No sooner had I applied my powders when a wyrm *eight feet long* and *thick as a serpente* leapt out of Mr. Stiles' throate, and the lady was a widow no longer."

A worthless patent cure.

Dr. Puddle's handbill.

George Puddle, a peculiar in the fifteenth century, could cure all sorts of eye problems, including blindness, and claimed he had once been blind himself. His pamphlet told this incredible story: "I have wrought a wonderful cure upon an unfortunate thiefe who broke into the wrong house by night. First he was struck down with a rod of iron, then his face was battered and flatted, his hair twisted from his head, and with thumbs placed in both eyes they were by violence forced out. In this barbarous state he was brought to me, yet by my expertise I replaced his eyes and restored him to perfect sight again. This being notoriously known to the whole city and all gentlemen and ladies here. I also repair eyeglasses!"

His claims were a bit *too* miraculous, and in failing to properly disguise his peculiar talents, he ran afoul of the authorities. He was hauled before a tribunal, charged with "diabolical instigation" and "practicing the execrable arts," then boiled alive in the street.

AS GRAVEDIGGERS AND DEATH WORKERS

Much peculiarness is tolerated in the death-adjacent trades. Gravediggers, embalmers, cremators, and other such night-workers are relegated to the shadows by a society that would rather look away. It is assumed that strange people gravitate naturally to strange professions. But don't let this give you a false sense of security; just because people don't want to look at you doesn't mean they can't see you.

The fate of young Ernie Childress makes a suitable cautionary tale. A cemetery groundskeeper employed him to sweep the stones, remove wilted flowers, etc. Ernie was a lonely boy and also a talented dead-riser, and he preferred the company and conversation of the recently deceased to the living. One day a bereaved woman saw Ernie walking through the graveyard with her husband, who'd been dead not three days, talking and laughing in a most animated way—all in broad daylight. She ran from the place in hysterics, returning with a gang of armed men. None believed that she had seen her husband walking and talking, but nevertheless they found Ernie lunching in a crypt filled with open coffins, the bodies all disturbed as if they'd been sitting upright and chatting with him just a minute earlier. Ernie was assumed to be a grave-robbing ghoul. The mob spared his life because of his tender age, but he was committed for the rest of his days to an asylum.

The unfortunate Ernie Childress.

AS PRETERNATURALLY GIFTED HOMICIDE DETECTIVES

Not a few clairvoyantly talented peculiars have made careers for themselves as homicide detectives.

Peculiar detective Rick McCloskey knew just where to drag the lake.

AS MAGICIANS

Onlookers assume they are being tricked.

AS PROPHETS, SHAMANS, AND OTHER INTERMEDIARIES BETWEEN THE SACRED AND THE SECULAR

Not to be confused with spirit mediums or tent-revival charlatans, these peculiars are truly convinced that they are gifted with—or burdened with—a connection to the divine. They may well be; we take no official stance on religion other than to say it is beyond our ken. A word of warning, though: Prophets are nearly always considered unwelcome disruptors of the established order, so if you choose this life (or if it chooses you), be ready for a world of trouble.

IN A CIRCUS SIDESHOW

Traveling sideshows once provided shelter and employment for peculiars the world over. At the height of the sideshow's popularity in the late nineteenth century,

Sideshows have been a mainstay of employment for peculiars hiding in plain sight.

fully half their performers were peculiar. Unfortunately, changing social mores and the rise of television eventually doomed the sideshow, depriving many who were unemployable elsewhere of their livelihoods.

HERE ARE SOME FAMOUS PECULIAR SIDESHOW ARTISTS:

Arachnagirl worked in Berlin's infamous *Monstrositätenshow*. For ten pfennig, customers viewed her "dance of the web." But for a deutschmark they were allowed behind the screen, where from the neck down she was all spider. It's said she hatched over five hundred children, every one of them normal.

Arachnagirl.

"Walter Wentworth, 75 years old, and for many years a professional contortionist, is in New York looking for someone to buy his body. He has long been a wonder to medical men on account of the wonderful pliability of his frame, which he has already sold twice— once to Dr. Cowes of Detroit, and later to Dr. Wilder of New York, receiving in each case $100. Both these medical men are dead and now Wentworth is looking for a third speculator." —*Brooklyn Daily Eagle,* April 28, 1900

Walter Wentworth, contortionist.

"Headless" Jim Buckmann, a peculiar dissocio who could detach his head from his body at will, made his living shocking audiences at tent shows with demonstrations like the one advertised below. A nurse was on duty at each of his performances to check the blood pressure of audience members before the show began. At the surprising climax, an "executioner" would give his horrible torture contraption a final, pitiless wrench, and old Jim's head would pop off and roll, grinning and cackling, into the horrified crowd. Then he would rise, calmly retrieve his head, and all those who hadn't fainted would hand over their ten-cent fee.

A hand-painted advertisement for "Headless" Jim Buckmann's horrifying show.

Thumbelina was a living doll who began her sideshow career as a ventriloquist's puppet, but after some years her dignity could no longer withstand such humiliations. She flipped the act on its head and began hypnotizing both the ventriloquist and volunteers from their audiences to use as *her* puppets. This brought her some success and not a little fame, and she began to receive top billing above even the lion tamers and fire-eaters. One fire-eater in particular grew jealous of her celebrity and told a big top crowd in Turkey Scratch, Arkansas, that Thumbelina was possessed by the Demon Lord Baal. They stormed the stage in the middle of her act and tore her limb from limb. Her head was saved by the terrified ventriloquist, and later found its way to a display box in Myron Bentham's ersatz museum. They say that now and then her eyes still open of their own accord, but she never speaks.

Thumbelina (right) and her puppet (left).

FOCUS ON:
Halloween

Most people think Halloween began as an ancient pagan festival, but that's merely a cover story. Peculiars invented it long ago as a holiday of convenience: an annual opportunity to walk unnoticed among normals. It's the one day of the year when we don't have to dress up or disguise ourselves; we can simply breathe a sigh of relief and be ourselves.

Normal or peculiar? On Halloween, only an ymbryne can tell.

On Halloween, anachronistic styles of dress are perfectly acceptable. Extra limbs will be explained away as prosthetics, and so on. If you feel more comfortable wearing a mask for added anonymity, no one will question you. It's also a day when, historically, our enemies take a holiday from hunting us, as it's much more difficult to tell normals from peculiars.

This crude mask allows a young peculiar to conceal his forty-nine eyeballs.

Entrance to Miss Finfoot's loop, inside a petrol station decorated for Halloween.

This is why more loops are made on Halloween than any other day. Miss Finfoot's loop in Essex, 1955, Miss Trumpeter's loop in Cork, Ireland, 1976, and Miss Woodhen's loop in St. Andrews, Scotland, 1993, are all on October 31.

Halloween is a particular relief for invisibles, who can wear costumes that cover their entire bodies without raising alarm.

The Dangers of Exposure

I have attempted to describe ways a peculiar might pass safely and quickly through the present, or even live there undetected for a protracted length of time. But perhaps I have put the hearse before the grimbear, and prescribed a remedy before first describing the disease. Why, after all, do we need to hide in the first place? Why must so many of us live in time loops? If we were to simply leave them, and live undisguised among normals, would the result really be so dreadful?

Yes, Dear Reader. It would be decidedly, singularly, extraordinarily, apocalyptically dreadful. Here, as always, history is the best teacher. It gives us many examples of how quickly things can go "teats up" when peculiars are exposed.

Normals fear what they do not understand, and fear is a cancer that can quickly metastasize into hatred and violence. Occasionally, peculiars who reveal themselves and live openly among normals get lucky: They are dismissed as mad, but harmless, and ignored. More often than not, though, exposed peculiars are assumed to be witches, warlocks, demons,

Some unlucky ancestors.

or otherwise allied with dark forces. Uncountable numbers have been killed in witch hunts. Between 1580 and 1630, some ten thousand people were burned at the stake in Europe alone, an alarming percentage of whom were peculiar.

Regrettably, we make convenient scapegoats. Whenever some problem afflicts a community of normals and the cause is uncertain, known or suspected peculiars are often the first to be blamed. We have been held responsible for outbreaks of plague, poisoned wells, ships lost at sea, abnormal births, natural disasters, financial misfortunes, and such petty tribulations as disagree-

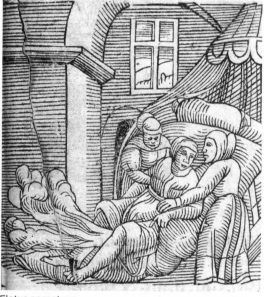

able weather, bland food, and gastrointestinal problems. That's no exaggeration: a 1656 witch trial in Iceland saw peculiar Jón Jónsson accused of using a magical book and farting runes (*fretrúnir*) to curse a girl who'd spurned him "with crapulence and wind unending," as the official charges against him read. Her distress continued day and night

Flatus perpetuus.

for weeks, causing her terrible embarrassment and abdominal pain, and prompting her new fiancé to break off their engagement. The girl's father filed suit against Jón, fabricating magical runes as evidence, and Jón was tortured until he confessed to the crime of sorcery. He was no sorcerer, of course, but a jealous and petty peculiar who was indeed guilty of afflicting the girl with chronic flatus—and subsequently everyone in the village who attended his burning. As the flames consumed him, he used his last words to forever blight them: "*May the turf beneath your bottom scorch, may your breeches be torn asunder, may your intestines erupt with stinking flame!*" Within days the villagers of Kirkjubol had abandoned their houses, never to return, and wherever they went they were treated as noisome pariahs. To this day, Icelanders refer to a bad case of gas as "Jónsson's curse."

"Sezt nidr ok rod runar
Ris upp ok fis vid!
Einfalt vid trollum vid pu."

"Sit down and interpret the runes; rise up and fart!
Your ass will announce trouble for you."

Peculiars who fall in love with a normal (against all sage advice; see the tragic tale of Gloria, page 94) naturally wish they could reveal themselves to the object of their affection, but be warned: This is a terrible mistake. Even normals who profess to love you unconditionally may lose their wits when confronted with your true nature.

WHAT TO DO
┈┈➔ IF YOU ARE EXPOSED ◆┈┈

If you can convince the normals who saw you that they didn't see what they thought they saw, do so and then quickly leave the scene.
If that's not possible:

1. Run away.

2. Make sure you aren't followed.

3. Return to the safety of a loop . . . *without* leading normals to its entrance.

4. Tell an ymbryne.

5. Fill out a form P-14, Exposure Incident Report (below), and give it to your ymbryne. She will file it with the Office of Normal Affairs, who will decide whether an Official Intercession is needed, and/or memory-wipes for the normal witnesses.

6. You may be censured if your conduct in the present is deemed reckless. Disciplinary actions can include loss of travel privileges, browbeating, stern lectures, interminable lectures, and in cases where intentional malice is determined, incarceration in a punishment loop.

- -

EXPOSURE INCIDENT REPORT
[FORM P-14]

Name of peculiars involved _____

Exposure date and location _____

Brief description of incident _____
_____

Number of normal witnesses _____

Were police summoned? CIRCLE: Y / N

Were you photographed or otherwise recorded? CIRCLE: Y / N

Any deaths? If so, list cause(s) and number_____

_____

Are you ashamed of yourself? CIRCLE: Y / N OR N/A

IF YOU ARE
····→ PURSUED BY A MOB ←····

CIRCLE YOUR ANSWERS BELOW.

QUESTION ONE: How inflamed are they?
- ➺ Merely peeved
- ➺ Rather irate
- ➺ Downright murderous

> *IF MURDEROUS, SKIP TO RESPONSE THREE.*
> *OTHERWISE, CONTINUE ON TO QUESTION TWO.*

QUESTION TWO: What are they wielding?
- ➺ Brooms
- ➺ Cellular telephones
- ➺ Clubs
- ➺ Torches

> *IF CLUBS OR TORCHES, SKIP TO RESPONSE THREE.*
> *OTHERWISE, CONTINUE ON TO QUESTION THREE.*

QUESTION THREE: Are they shouting anything intelligible?
- ➺ "Let us take your photograph."
- ➺ "What a delightful footrace."
- ➺ "Stop so we can club you."
- ➺ "Die, monster, die."

> *IF ONE OF THE LATTER TWO, SKIP TO RESPONSE THREE.*
> *OTHERWISE, EMPLOY RESPONSE ONE OR TWO.*

RESPONSE ONE: Run faster.

RESPONSE TWO: You may have inadvertently joined a marathon. Stop running immediately; unnecessary exercise is a waste of the vertiferous humors.

RESPONSE THREE: You are permitted to use any means at your disposal to save yourself. While we can't encourage you to dazzle them with further displays of peculiarity, it may be necessary. In the words of the peculiar poet Arthur Clough: "*Thou shalt not kill; but need'st not strive / Officiously to keep alive.*"

····➔ EXPOSURE EVENTS WHICH ◆····
REQUIRED OFFICIAL INTERCESSION

THE WAR OF THE OAKEN BUCKET

The oldest ymbrynes remember the disastrous Italian war of 1325. Two peculiar factions rose up against each other, and the battle raged not only across physical borders, but also temporal ones. The peculiars fought in loops, and the fighting spilled into the present. Scores of peculiars died, and thousands of normals. An entire city was burned to the ground. So many normals witnessed the fighting that there was no containing it. It sparked a pogrom against our kind, a bloody purge that drove peculiars out of Northern Italy for a century. It took an enormous effort to recover. We had to memory-wipe a great many people. We even enlisted peculiar scholars, the famous Perplexus Anomalous among them, to revise normal history books, so that the carnage would be remembered as something other than the War of the Freaks, which is what it was called for generations. Finally, Perplexus and his scholars were able to rewrite it as "The War of the Oaken Bucket." To this day normals still believe thousands died battling over a wooden pail.

MASSACHUSETTS GIRL PHOTOGRAPHED CLOBBERING A POLICEMAN

Prior to the rise of photography and mass media, exposure incidents were easier to cover up. We have to be more careful now. Even a small incident can cause a great deal of trouble if one of the normal witnesses is armed with a camera. One such episode involved a peculiar girl caught shoplifting in Quincy, Massachusetts, in 1937.

Pauline Giamatti was convicted of reckless exhibition and sentenced to three years of stern lectures.

Apprehended and handcuffed, the girl, gifted with peculiar strength, simply flipped the arresting officer over her shoulder like a sack of soiled laundry and ran off with him. A crowd gave chase, as well as several more officers. She surely would've been shot if she hadn't been so small and seemingly young. Rather than murder her way out of the fracas, she wisely allowed the police to arrest her. Ymbrynes intervened and secured her release; that was the easy bit. The sticky thing was explaining the incident in the press, a problem made all the more challeng-

How the imbeciles were persuaded.

ing because it had been photographed. A ridiculous cover story was fed to the newspapers involving hypnosis and mind control, and fortunately the public believed it. The officers involved were discreetly memory-wiped.

THE BOY WHO FELL INTO THE SKY

My ward Olive Abroholos Elephanta was lighter than air from the minute she was born: She floated out of her mother and straight up to the ceiling, whereupon the woman fainted from both exhaustion and shock. While her ashamed parents were able to keep her peculiarity secret until I adopted her, other gravitationally challenged children have not been so fortunate. Young Harald Beckner was one. Harald was lighter than Olive ever was, which made his life considerably more difficult. At –30 kg, even leaden shoes weren't sufficient to keep him ground-bound; he was forced to supplement his shoes with stones in his pockets, a coat lined with sewn-in sandbags, and a belt filled with crushed granite around his waist. He ate only the heaviest foods in an attempt to gain weight, to no avail; the older he got, the lighter he grew.

At night his parents allowed him to take off all his weights and sleep on a mattress and blankets they had nailed to the rafters. But one morning he woke up so groggy that he got out of bed, rolled straight out the window, and fell into the sky. He began to shout, attracting the attention of an early-rising farmer who raised a general alarm. Harald's peculiarity was such that his weight increased with altitude, and he reached equilibrium at about eight thousand feet. The scene caused quite a stir. There he floated, high above the town with no way to get down. All the neighbors came out to gawk. The local authorities dispatched an airship to retrieve him, and by late afternoon he was returned, shivering but alive, to his family.

Hundreds of people had witnessed it. Some were convinced he was either a fairy or a demon, and his parents packed him up and left town the

The whole town witnessed the boy's fall upward.

How they fetched him.

next day. Hushing things up was a massive undertaking. But rather than quickly memory-wiping everyone in the town, which might have created its own problems (imagine the headlines: THE TOWN THAT FORGOT TUESDAY!), ymbrynes wiped the most hysterical witnesses first, then others, one or two per day, so that gradually, over the course of years, the incident faded into a kind of poorly remembered urban legend. People still talk about the boy who fell into the sky, but few believe he actually existed.

HEAD OF THE CLASS

Kate and Bess were dissocios—peculiars whose heads could be harmlessly removed from their bodies, then reattached with little trouble. Unfortunately, they were also compulsive pranksters, and one day decided to switch heads with each other and attend school like that to see if anyone would notice. No one did—until Kate's head, which had been shoddily attached with staples, popped loose and rolled onto her desk in the middle of home economics class. Half the students fainted, making them fairly easy to memory-wipe, but the rest had to be tracked down one by one, which was no easy task.

Showing off again.

YMBRYNES

> "Whatever else is unsure
> in this stinking dunghill of a world,
> an ymbryne's devotion is not."
>
> —ENOCH O'CONNOR, MISQUOTING J. JOYCE

All peculiardom would be diminished if any of our types were to vanish, but there is only one type of peculiar we could not survive without: the ymbryne. I say this not to boast. Though I am deeply proud to be an ymbryne, the mantle of ymbrynehood is a heavy one I sometimes wish I could set down. But without the protection we offer, peculiars would have been hunted to extinction long ago. To be born with the powers of an ymbryne is to inherit a terrible and awesome responsibility, one that nobody is permitted to shirk. It is the only peculiarity that binds one by law to perform certain duties. If we are the most powerful and important of peculiars, we are also the least free.

There are a few traits common to all ymbrynes. All ymbrynes are women. All can shape-shift into bird form,[7] each of us a

---

7.   In the distant past, we were more bird than human, though that has reversed over time. The first ymbryne was a goshawk who discovered she could turn into a human. Her story is told in "The First Ymbryne," one of the *Tales of the Peculiar*.

An ymbryne and her wards keep the watch.

An ymbryne out shopping with her young assistant (holding basket).

different species. (There is no other peregrine ymbryne, for instance, nor will there ever be while I am alive.) All of us can create time loops. Most can wipe the memories of normals. Some ymbrynes have additional peculiarities besides, like Miss Blackbird, whose third eye operates independently from the other two, but those talents are incidental and usually minor.

It is the responsibility of each ymbryne, once properly trained and having graduated from the Ymbryne Academy, to maintain a time loop for the protection of peculiar children.[8] She must sustain her loop, resetting it daily, and ensure her wards are fed, clothed, educated, and prevented from wandering into the present unsupervised. Several times each year she makes scouting trips to search for new, undiscovered peculiar children who may require help. She is also expected to take part in sessions of peculiar government, traveling now and then for meetings of the Council of Ymbrynes or other ministerial bodies in which she may be tasked to participate.

In other words, we have so many roles to fulfill, it's a good thing we

---

8. Peculiar adults are also allowed to live in ymbrynes' loops, but they are not given priority, and their number is capped. This is because peculiar children require special attention and lessons, and benefit more from the company of their peers. Adults live in separate loops that are usually denser and more populous.

need only an hour or two of sleep each night. Occasionally, an overtaxed ymbryne might take on an assistant, usually a young ymbryne-in-training sent by the academy for a period of mentorship.

Ymbrynes exist all over the world, as do peculiars, and there are ymbryne councils in Africa and Asia, for instance, which operate in parallel to our own. We occasionally receive ambassa-

Miss Turaco giving a lesson on peculiar genetics.

dors and emissaries from these councils, but since the rise of the wights and their hollowgast, we have been cut off from much of the world, prevented from traveling far from home, and forced to focus mainly on the security of our loops and wards here. One day, should external threats abate, it would be wonderful to establish stronger ties with ymbrynes from faraway places. In my view, a global alliance of peculiars could only

make us stronger and more resistant to threats like the hollows.

Traditionally, ymbrynes do not marry and are discouraged from having children, so that we are never tempted to favor a biological child—who, in all likelihood, would not be peculiar—over our adopted ones. In the Far East, some ymbrynes wear wedding clothes as a symbol that they are married to their work.

Miss Palapitta's wedding attire symbolizes devotion to her work.

At 304 years of age, Miss Verdin is among the oldest living ymbrynes.

The dormitory hall at Miss Avocet's Ymbryne Academy.

That was my window, top-right above the shrubbery!
I shared a room with Miss Cuckoo, my dear friend.
We snuck out so often, Miss Avocet was finally
forced to nail the window shut.
We got into such devilry ...

The Ymbryne Academy

M iss Avocet's Ymbryne Academy has trained all of Europe's ymbrynes for the past century and a half. The program is rigorous and unrelenting. Coursework can take ten years or longer, depending on the aptitude of the student, and culminates in an apprenticeship under a working ymbryne and an ambitious final thesis project. Only the most talented and dedicated students will graduate to become full-fledged ymbrynes. Some find the program so daunting they drop out after a short time, while others, despite diligent work, lack certain talents and are judged better equipped to fill a supporting role in one of the peculiar ministries.

Ymbrynes-in-training practice at conjuring a loop.

A young recruit immersed in her studies.

Dressed in graduation day regalia.

Spring

Shape-shifting lessons.

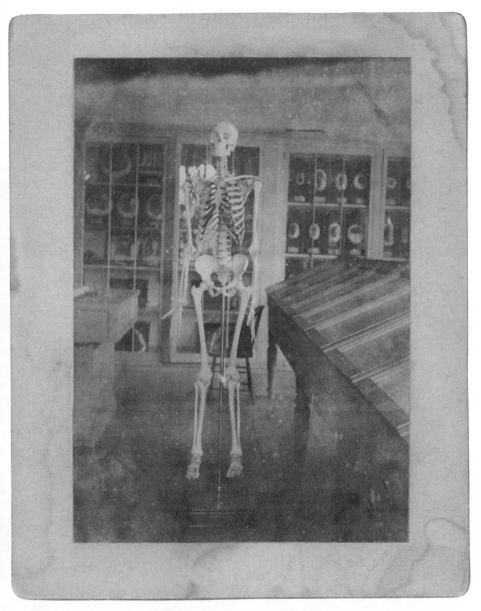

Mister Tempus, the mascot and official class monitor of the first-years.

*Mister Tempus was rarely at his post,
so frequently was he stolen by pranksters.
Ah, youth* ...

Demi-Ymbrynes and Lesser Time Manipulators

Ymbrynes are not the only peculiars who can manipulate time. There are those born with a portion of our gift; they lack the ability to create time loops, but can reset and maintain them, for example. These time-manipulating peculiars take various forms and are known by many names.

Demi-ymbrynes have long functioned as stand-ins for full ymbrynes in America, whose peculiars have

This demi-ymbryne kept the ymbryne she ousted locked in a cage.

Frequently late and invariably drunk, clock-winders are a last resort for loop maintenance.

been ruled by thuggish gangs since the early twentieth century. Loop-keepers can prevent loops from collapsing when even demi-ymbrynes cannot be found, though they are notoriously unreliable. Neither demi-ymbrynes nor clock-winders can shape-shift into birds, which makes it fairly straightforward for true ymbrynes to prove themselves.

This boy believed he could teach himself to adjust and reset loops without an ymbryne's help. Not long after this photo was taken, his untutored tinkering created a temporal sublunary divergence—which, naturally, turned his unlucky loop-mates into gelatinous goop.

Photography:
A Peculiar Art Form

"Normals have been trying to erase us
for centuries. Photography is a way to fix ourselves
in place. To prove we were here, and not
the monsters they made us out to be."

—EMMA BLOOM

You may have noticed, if you're new to peculiardom, that we have a special relationship with photography. Many of us are afflicted with some form of photo-mania, and there is a whole ministry within the peculiar government dedicated to documenting and cataloguing our people photographically. Part of our devotion to the craft can be traced to the fact that it was a peculiar, Louis Daguerre, who helped invent and popularize photography. Though it was quickly adopted around the world, Daguerre initially developed his daguerreotype process to document his fellow peculiars. (In fact, I met him once; he visited the Ymbryne Academy with his camera while I was a fledgling there.)

It's the rare ymbryne who doesn't keep treasured photos of her wards

tucked away in an album somewhere, and every ymbryne has at least an old Brownie box camera, if not a more elaborate setup involving glass plates and viewing hoods. We document our lives and those of our wards both to celebrate peculiarness and to preserve its memory for future generations, should the worst come to pass.

Daguerre, the father of photography—and a peculiar.

A young ymbryne with her all-important photo album.

Me as a fledgling with Miss Avocet, years ago. Photo by L. Daguerre.

Photo-mania afflicts many of us.

A traveling photographer, emissary of the Dept. of Photographic Records.

A PAGE FROM ONE OF MY ALBUMS

On the following pages you'll find a sample from one of my personal albums. The photos are from 1907, when I was an apprentice ymbryne working at a loop near Cheltenham. A peaceful time for us. We had no idea it was the calm before the storm.

I've sadly misplaced my old Kodak,
but Emma has taken on the role of famie
family historian in my place. I hope one
day she will assemble her photos in an album
even lovelier than the ones I grew up with

Leise is never without
her Kodak.

Jasper mastering the
voca spiritum ~
Edison's ghost phone.

Fritzie's doppelgänger
before it turned wicked.

Our loop entrance.

Another beautiful mourning.

An evening's entertainment.

Naughty Simon and his boneshaker, which he isn't supposed to ride in the house.

Robert lived in the mirror. This is how we brought him on picnics.

OUR ENEMIES

> "Sleep, little one, and rest your head
> Sleep and dream so sweetly
> For in the morning the fiends will come
> And a face looms at the window."
>
> —TRADITIONAL PECULIAR LULLABY

If we had only normals to vex us, life for peculiars would not be half as hard. The pogroms and witch-hunting manias we once endured are long past. Normals are easy enough to dupe. So long as we can fool them, they are as stupid and gentle as lambs.

But it isn't normals who keep ymbrynes awake at night. It isn't normals who haunt peculiar dreams, or populate our horror tales. No, the shadows of the world squirm with terrors much worse than that: ancient eyes forever searching for us, monstrous appendages aching to slice us open and pull out our souls. Our true enemies are not normal. Far from it: They are leagues more intelligent than that.

They are—or once were—just like us. And that makes them infinitely more dangerous.

Come now,
my child
if we were planning
to harm you, do you think
we'd be lurking here
beside the path
in the very dark-
est part of
the forest?

—KENNETH PATCHEN

The Hollowgast

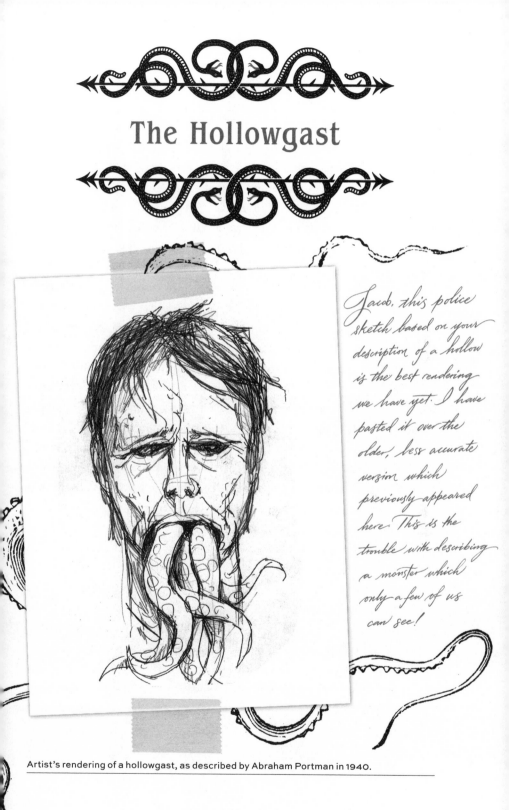

Jacob, this police sketch based on your description of a hollow is the best rendering we have yet. I have pasted it over the older, less accurate version which previously appeared here. This is the trouble with describing a monster which only a few of us can see!

Artist's rendering of a hollowgast, as described by Abraham Portman in 1940.

····→ ORIGINS ←····

Some years ago, around the turn of the last century, a splinter faction emerged among our people—a coterie of disaffected peculiars with dangerous ideas. They believed they had discovered a
method by which the unique qualities of time loops could be perverted
to confer upon them a kind of immortality; not merely the suspension of
aging, but the reversal of it. They promised their followers eternal youth
enjoyed outside the confines of loops, a life of jumping back and forth
from future to past with impunity, suffering none of the ill effects that
have always prevented such recklessness. In other words, mastering time
without being mastered by death. The whole notion was mad, a refuta-
tion of the empirical laws that govern everything.[9]

My two brothers, both technically brilliant but rather lacking in
sense, were consumed with this misguided idea. They even had the au-
dacity to request my assistance in making it a reality. I refused, of course,
but they would not be deterred. Having grown up among Miss Avocet's
ymbrynes-in-training, they knew more about our unique art than most
peculiar males. Just enough, I'm afraid, to be dangerous. Despite warnings, even threats, from the Council, in the summer of 1908 my brothers and several hundred members of their renegade faction ventured into
the Siberian wilderness to conduct their hateful experiment. For the site
they chose a nameless old permaloop uninhabited for centuries. We expected them to return within a week, tails between their legs, humbled
by the immutable nature of nature. Instead, their comeuppance was far
more dramatic: a catastrophic explosion that rattled windows as far as
the Azores. Anyone within three hundred miles surely thought it was the
end of the world. We assumed they'd all been killed, that obscene world-
cracking bang their last collective utterance.

We were mistaken. They survived, in a manner of speaking. Others might call the state of being they subsequently assumed a kind of
living damnation. Weeks later there began a series of attacks upon

---

9. There have since been some promising developments in the field of age reversal, though their results
are not yet conclusive, and even if such controversial techniques prove effective, they could never entirely
eliminate the dangers or cost of living in time loops.

peculiars by awful creatures who, apart from their shadows, could not be seen except by peculiars specially attuned to them.*These were our first clashes with the hollowgast. It was some time before we realized that the tentacle-mawed abominations were in fact our wayward brothers, crawled from the smoking crater left behind by their experiment. Rather than becoming gods, they had transformed themselves into devils.

What went wrong is still a matter of debate. One theory is that they reverse-aged themselves to a time before even their souls had been conceived, which is why we called them *hollowgast*—"empty souls."

In a cruel twist of irony, they did achieve the immortality they'd been seeking. It's believed that the hollows can live thousands of years. But it is a life of constant physical torment, humiliating debasement, and insatiable hunger for the flesh of their former kin.

····→ PHYSICAL DESCRIPTION ←····

Because hollowgast are visible only to a gifted few, we rely on those individuals to describe the hollow's appearance. Invariably, the picture they paint is a monstrous corruption of the human form: the face corpselike and gray; eyepits black and dripping a viscous, corrosive liquid; the back acutely hunched; the flesh hanging loose from its frame like a suit several sizes too large; the colossal mouth packed with a squirming trio of muscular, tentaclelike tongues that can whip out and drag victims into its powerful jaws, which are crowded with twice the normal number of teeth, each one sharp as a sword.

A walking nightmare, to be sure.

*Most famously your grandfather, who was not yet born and wouldn't join our ranks for another three decades.

➤➤ Being invisible, a hollowgast is often announced by its scent—it reeks of putrefaction—and by its unique tri-tongued shadow.

➤➤ A hollow can smell your peculiarity, and can sense peculiar abilities being used from a distance. If you suspect one might be close, *do not use your ability or it will be drawn directly to you.*

➤➤ Hollows cannot enter loops. This is a key reason loops have become our preferred refuge for the past century, and more necessary than ever to our survival. *Unfortunately no longer the case*

➤➤ The eyes seem to be the most vulnerable part of a hollowgast's body. A sharp object plunged deeply enough into one of the ocular sockets will usually dispatch the creature. Getting close enough to achieve this without being strangled by its tongues or mangled in its jaws is another matter, and one best left to professional hollow-hunters.

Peculiar necropologist Shintaro Nomura at the site of a hollowgast feeding frenzy.

ANSWERS TO QUESTIONS
·····→ ABOUT HOLLOWGAST ←·····
FREQUENTLY ASKED BY CHILDREN

Q: Can hollows talk?

A: They can be spoken to, in a special dialect, by their wightish masters and a few talented peculiars. But they do not seem to talk back, nor to speak to one another. They are not social creatures and do not congregate naturally in packs. They have no interest in community or friendship or any pleasure at all other than prying open your skull to slurp out the brains inside.

Q: If I'm disguised as a normal, can they find me outside my loop?

A: They can smell peculiars and could find you in a crowd of ten thousand normals.

Q: Do hollowgast go about naked?

A: Children seem unaccountably fascinated by this, and should be ashamed of themselves.

Q: Do they know where I live?

A: Probably.

Q: Can they get me when I am sleeping?

A: Especially then.

If you've the time, Jacob, it would be most useful to have a written account of your brief time in a hollowgast den.

Q: If they get me, will they eat me right away?

A: Sometimes they drag their victims back to burrows or dens they've made and hold them there for a while, like a squirrel gathering nuts for winter.

Q: Do hollows dream of rotting sheep?

A: Hollows rarely sleep, and when they do, they dream only of removing your soft, palpitating heart from its bone-cage.

HOW TO DEFEND YOURSELF
·····➔ AGAINST a HOLLOWGAST ◂·····

The official recommendation of the Ymbryne Council and the Committee for the Study of Practical Protections Against Hollowgast Attack is to *RUN AWAY IMMEDIATELY* should you encounter one. However, that has not prevented various groups from attempting to form Hollowgast Defense Leagues, usually with tragic results.

Another nightmare.

Some groups persevered longer than others, but after extensive train-

ing and experiments with different types of weaponry, each was ultimately disbanded after an inevitably disastrous engagement with actual hollows. That they couldn't see the monsters they were supposed to be fighting was ever the insurmountable problem.

The only group to have any true success was Abraham Portman's network of hollow-hunters. Abe had the exceptionally rare gift—though he often called it a curse—of being able to see hollowgast. He honed

Willy Winkleveiss's Alpine League pioneered the use of crossbows against hollowgast.

Famed hollowgast-hunter Abraham Portman.

Did Abe ever talk to you about the cell or his war years? Harrowing and inspiring stuff. He was truly an amazing man——.

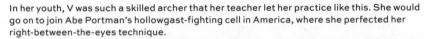

In her youth, V was such a skilled archer that her teacher let her practice like this. She would go on to join Abe Portman's hollowgast-fighting cell in America, where she perfected her right-between-the-eyes technique.

his hollow-killing techniques during the Second World War, during which he fought Nazis and hollowgast simultaneously, the former with the British Army and the latter in a specialized, secret cell of peculiars that later became a model for hollowgast defense. After the war, he moved to America and founded his own group of hollow-hunters with a small number who shared his talent. For most of the latter half of the twentieth century, they ran clandestine missions across America to kill hollowgast, disrupt the activities of wights, and rescue kidnapped peculiar children. Abe was kind enough to write and share his top tips for fighting hollows, in case running is not an option:

> If you're like most people and can't see hollows, get into a position where you can at least catch a glimpse of their shadow. The best is an open space with the sun behind your enemy, so the shadow gets thrown right in front of you. If it's nighttime (and it probably will be . . . they prefer hunting at night), find a floodlight or carry a strong flashlight with you. Attack from a distance if you can. Hollows are deadliest at close range. A compact crossbow is the best weapon: silent; portable; accurate; and if you know the right people, you can purchase exploding arrow-tips. Guns are second best, silenced if possible. Aim for the head. A hollow can lose both legs

and still chase you using its tongues as substitutes. Massive blood loss doesn't seem to affect them. Pikes, torches, and javelins are also good options if a crossbow or gun isn't available. Otherwise, I have listed alternate choices in order from most preferable to least: sword; spiked ball and chain; bat with nails in it; bat with no nails; long knife; short knife; boiling water; sharpened stick; letter opener; regular stick; your thumbs. If you can trap a hollow in a cell or a deep hole, it will starve to death in about a week, though its screams can attract a lot of attention. I've also had luck running them over with tanks, pushing them off the roofs of tall buildings, and feeding them dead goats stuffed with explosives (keep well clear of the detonation—a hollow's stomach acid can melt steel). Above all, be creative and have fun.

Testing an experimental anti-hollow nerve gas in 1936—a failure. Though a single whiff could melt human lung tissue, prolonged exposure only succeeded in giving the beasts hiccups.

Deanford Bash, expert in modern and medieval weapons, founder of the American Hollowgast Defense League. He was fatally mauled by a bear in 1928 (without ever having encountered a hollow).

The aftermath of the infamous SS *Avondale* tragedy, in which a hollowgast being transported across the English Channel for study escaped its chains and massacred all aboard.

The Wights

A pair of wights in disguise.

W hen a hollowgast has at last sated itself with peculiar souls, it transforms—gruesomely, over the course of some days, like a pupating insect emerging from its baggy flesh-cocoon—into a wight. Unlike hollows, wights are visible to all, can enter loops, and have no hidden mouth-tentacles or rows of sharp teeth. They are weak, possess no peculiar abilities, and are apparently normal in every respect save one: Their pupil-less eyes are blank as eggs. But what they lack in deadly mandibles they more than make up for with cunning intelligence and a chameleonlike mastery of disguise that helps them blend into normal society with ease. They scour the world for peculiars and our loops, often with a hungry hollowgast as their companion. Wights frequently travel with a hollowgast, with whom they have a mutually dependent relationship: The powerful hollow kills anything the wight tells it to, and the comparatively feeble but shrewd wight procures a constant supply of victims, preferably peculiar, for his monstrous companion to eat. But catering to such a voluminous appetite almost always leaves a trail, which is a liability we can exploit to track them. Have an unusual number of murders accompanied the uncanny new stranger in town? Are gnawed limbs being discovered here and there? Your stranger could be a wight with a peckish partner.

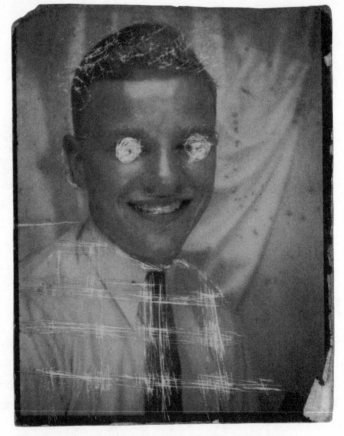

"The Man Who Visits Me at Dreamtime" by Billy, age eight.

The wights' goal is nothing less than the domination of peculiarkind, and subsequently all of humanity. I won't rehash their twisted philosophy here—suffice it to say wights are deeply biased against ymbrynes and believe we're largely to blame for the crimes perpetrated against peculiars over the centuries. We are too passive, they say, and have allowed peculiarkind to become weak and debased when we should be "claiming our place at the head of the human table." This is, of course, a pathetic power fantasy dreamed up by the fragile ego of a deeply insecure man—my embittered brother and the wights' leader, Caul—who never reconciled himself to the fact that he was a small, male cog in a society governed by powerful women. If implemented, his ideas would result in perpetual war and oceans of spilled blood. Nevertheless, his vision of peculiar dominance and promises of everlasting life attracted a sizable (and mostly male) following, and despite the fact that his failed plan turned them all into hollowgast, the wights are even more fanatically devoted to him now.

What follows is a necessarily incomplete list of known wights, accompanied by some brief identifying information. My hope is that by giving new peculiars some rough idea of the different guises wights have adopted in the past, they may better guard themselves in the future.

Jacob—though the wights and hollowgast are now much diminished, thanks in part to your own heroic actions—this remains essential material. The wights menaced us for more than a century, and are so cunning that I wouldn't be surprised if a number of them had slipped through the cracks and have merely gone underground, waiting for an opportunity to strike again. I fear some of those listed here may resurface one day. It's best to be prepared.

····➔ KNOWN WIGHTS ◆····
AND THEIR WHEREABOUTS

ALIASES: Joe Smith; Virgil Dante, Jr.

OCCUPATION: Traveling salesman

LAST SEEN: Cheltenham, UK

SUSPICIOUS BEHAVIORS: Buying vast quantities of meat from supermarkets; lurking about

STATUS: Presumed dead

If it's all right with you, I'd like to include an entry on Golan in the next edition of this book. The way he stalked you and Abe for years and the many aliases he used in doing so (neighbor, psychiatrist, bus driver, laborer, ornithologist, etc.) make him of particular interest. However, if you'd rather the wight responsible for your grandfather's death not be memorialized in these pages, I would understand. Let me know.

ALIAS: Dr. Wesley Bellichek

OCCUPATION: Visiting lecturer in anatomy at Oxford University, 1966–1975

SUSPICIOUS BEHAVIORS: "Dr. Bellichek always had the freshest cadavers," writes former student Amy S. "No one could figure out where he was getting them . . . until he was arrested."

FURTHER NOTES: Bellichek was feeding his hollow with grave-robbed bodies and using the leftovers to further his career. His academic post was merely an excuse to sniff around the university for late-blooming peculiars.

STATUS: He was broken out of jail in dramatic fashion shortly after his arrest—aided by an invisible accomplice who broke down the doors, bent the bars of his cell, and flung the guards down a stairwell.

He remains at large!

ALIAS: Karl Gunderson

OCCUPATION: Pig farmer; ax murderer

LAST-KNOWN DOMICILE: The precise middle of the Black Forest, Germany

SUSPICIOUS BEHAVIORS: Midnight digging; never letting anyone see what's inside his barn

STATUS: Jailed in the Lochranza Castle punishment loop

ALIAS: Unknown

OCCUPATION: Drifter; railroad switchyard operator

PECULIAR-HUNTING TACTICS: Has been known to detain long-distance passenger trains on the basis of fabricated mechanical issues while his hollowgast creeps from car to car, nosing for peculiars.

STATUS: ~~At large~~ *Killed in the first battle of Devil's Acre.*

ALIAS: Florence Atterton

OCCUPATION: School principal

LAST SEEN: Disappearing beneath the silty mud of Regent's Canal

PECULIAR-HUNTING TACTICS: Primary and secondary schools are fertile ground for peculiar-hunting, as this is the age when many peculiars manifest their abilities for the first time. All a wight like Miss Atterton has to do is keep watch for strangely gifted students, then steal them without attracting attention. Miss Atterton was typical of many school lurkers: She never stayed in one district for more than a year or two, as too many disappearances would raise suspicion. She was unusual in that she kept three hollowgast, not just one, but their voracious appetite for the student body (no pun intended) finally got Miss Atterton caught.

STATUS: Escaped from a life sentence on the Steamship *Chunder* punishment loop *[photo courtesy Dept. of Corrections and Retribution]*

····→ BEWARE THESE COMMON ←····
WIGHT DISGUISES

W ights are drawn to occupations that allow them to interact with large numbers of children and screen them for peculiarity. For instance, department-store Santas get close to streams of young people—though only for a few weeks of each year. Dentists and barbers see fewer of them, but they do it year-round and with sharp objects close at hand. School photographers are invited to study hundreds of young people every day, and the negatives can end up in the wights' own archives. Party clowns aren't as popular as they once were, but at one point in the mid-1950s, they were responsible for half of the kidnappings of peculiar children in America.

The last-known photo of young Anna Wakely.

A snip here, a snip there.

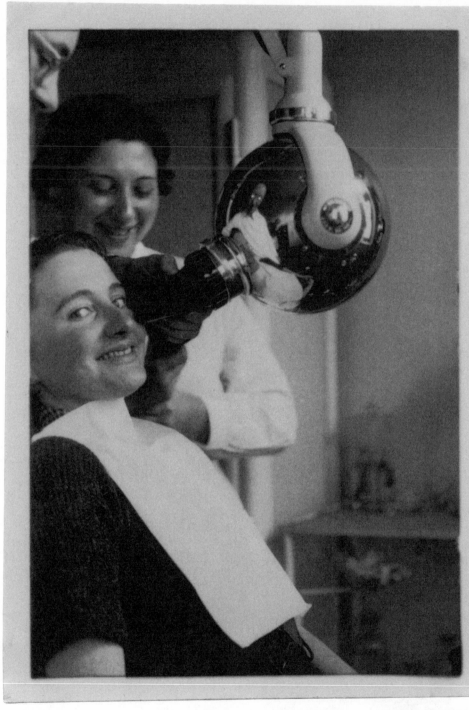

"You won't feel a thing.

"Say cheese, children."

After Abe Portman captured Crunchy the Clown, he found a hollowgast in the back of Crunchy's windowless white van.

····→ AN INVENTORY OF UNFORTUNATES: ←····
VICTIMS OF THE WIGHTS AND THEIR NIGHT-BEASTS

T hough many have fallen to our enemies, I include here a fragmentary catalogue of the lost in order to give them names and faces and to illustrate a few of the diverse ways peculiar children have run afoul of the wights. Let each be a reminder to watch your step, move through the world like a whisper, and be miserly with your confidences, lest your likeness appear here in the next edition of this book.

Should you recognize any of the children pictured below,
please contact an ymbryne immediately.

NAME: Egbert "Eggie" Nupkins

LAST SEEN: Delivering newspapers to the only house left standing in a desolate part of town, Hobo's Landing, Missouri.

STATUS: Disappeared

NAME: Anastasia Chernyskevsky

LAST SEEN: Walking in the woods with her flock of sheep in the great dark woods outside of Minsk. The sheep were discovered wandering and alone; snakelike drag marks along the path they followed point to a hollowgast attack.

STATUS: Bereft of life, extinguished, demised

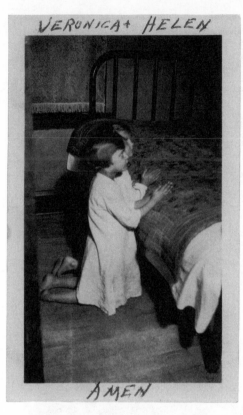

NAMES: Veronica and Helen Kennedy

LAST SEEN: Asleep in their beds, in the non-peculiar Catholic boarding school where they lived, in Ames, Iowa. In the morning they were gone, though the doors to the school were locked and there was no sign of any window having been opened. The police assumed the two were hiding somewhere in the building and searched every inch of it, to no avail. The girls reappeared two weeks later, disoriented, wearing rough clothing made from animal skins, and speaking in a language that only the sisters themselves could understand. They would not respond to questions in English.

They had, it seemed, forgotten it.

Years later, after relearning some of their native tongue, they described that night: they were levitated out of their beds and through a skylight window, where they met a "man with silver eyes" who led them to a "field full of light and children," where they lived for quite a long time, they said.

In their old age, in the asylum where they lived out the rest of their lives, they were the subject of an academic study. The professor of ancient languages who examined them died in a mysterious fire before he could publish his findings, but one of Abraham Portman's operatives was able to retrieve his papers from a fireproof safe in his burned office. He had proved that the girls returned speaking Gaulish. This was, of course, impossible: Gaulish had been extinct since AD 600.

No firm conclusion can be drawn from these curious events—only theories. But all agree that the girls were kidnapped by wights and involved in some fiendish experiment.

STATUS: Removed to a loop, where they live today in peaceful seclusion

NAME: Damian "Puff" Squirrley

LAST SEEN: Waiting outside a Piggly Wiggly grocery store while his ymbryne, Miss Shrike, shopped inside. Damian—physical age eight, true age fifty-seven—loved to smoke a pipe, and it's thought that the wight who took him trained his hollowgast to sniff out, from miles away, the unusual tobacco blend that Damian favored. When Miss Shrike came outside, she found Damian gone and a small disposable camera on the ground where he'd been standing, with this image exposed on the film inside. Wights have been known to leave such calling cards.

STATUS: Damian's peculiarity involved blowing out much more smoke than he took in, and he was able to create vast smokescreens. Shortly after his abduction, Ditch pirates in Devil's Acre began using a similar technique to disorient victims and escape detection. We believe Damian's soul was harvested and distilled into vials of Ambrosia for use by Caul's mercenaries.

NAME: Jerome Byersley

LAST SEEN: Broken Arrow, Oklahoma.

CIRCUMSTANCES OF HIS DISAPPEARANCE: Jerome possessed a peculiar mentalism that was well suited to reconstructing crime scenes and identifying perpetrators. Despite warnings from his ymbryne not to involve himself in normal affairs, he could often be seen riding his compact bicycle from one murder scene to another in order to aid local detectives. Unfortunately, his talent earned him a bit of celebrity, which attracted the attention of some unsavory characters. A murder was staged in order to lure him out of his loop, and he was snatched by a wight posing as a police detective.

STATUS: Missing

NAME: Charity Swidger

LAST SEEN: In her loop in Nineveh, Indiana, in the old hearse that is her bedroom.

CIRCUMSTANCES OF HER DISAPPEARANCE: Charity was a perfectly average young peculiar until she was snatched by wights while running an errand outside her loop. What happened next was most bizarre: her two abductors had no hollowgast with them and wanted to hold her captive until one arrived. With few good hiding places nearby, they devised a devilish prison for her: a large, ventilated glass box buried several feet in the ground and covered over with dirt. An air tube leading to the surface allowed her to breathe, and a small battery-powered lamp and a few comic books were provided for her entertainment. She was also given water and food, both laced with sedatives. When she didn't return after a few hours, her ymbryne went searching for her, frightening the wights away. She was finally discovered two weeks later when a boy walking through the woods heard singing coming from Charity's air tube. She was dehydrated and had aged forward thirty-five years, but she was alive and seemingly cheerful. When asked how she maintained such a positive attitude throughout her ordeal, Charity replied—in song—that *"Any time's kissing time, for my love and me / At deepest darkest midnight hour, he's all the light I need!"* (She had clearly lost her mind.) For the rest of her life, she could only sleep inside glass boxes and could only communicate in the form of musical numbers from turn-of-the-century show tunes.

STATUS: Damaged and strange

NAME: Altagracia Cortez

LAST SEEN: At her birthday party, Saltillo, Coahuila State, Mexico, with the infamous mime and suspected wight El Silencio.

STATUS: Missing

NAME: Courtice Pounds

LAST SEEN: Walking with a friend on Main Street in Staunton, Virginia.

CIRCUMSTANCES OF DISAPPEARANCE: Courtice could make herself disappear at will. A companion relates that they were attacked by a hollowgast, and in her terror Courtice disappeared to a degree from which she could not recover, a condition known in the invisible community as dissubstantiation. She is alive and well but cannot be seen except in the strongest light nor heard without special amplification, and only with immense physical effort can she exert so much as a featherlight touch upon an object. To capture her on film required a fourteen-minute exposure, during which she was temporarily paralyzed with the poison from a Japanese fugu fish in order to keep absolutely still.

STATUS: Insubstantial

····→ A PECULIAR ←····
"PENNY DREADFUL"

Storytelling has always played an important role in peculiar society—one only has to flip through the *Tales of the Peculiar* for evidence of that—and more than a few of us fancy ourselves writers. Lately, a chilling new type of fiction has become popular with our wards: stories written about wights, detailing their lives, habits, and hunting expeditions. Of course, these are particulars we can only guess at and which are no doubt exaggerated for sensational effect, but that has not stopped our less scrupulous authors from scribbling away at these dreadful potboilers. They do a hot trade on the peculiar gray market and have been made all the more popular because a few ymbrynes have attempted (foolishly, I think) to ban them. Though they can be needlessly titillating, I say there's nothing wrong with attempting to imagine the world from our enemies' perspective. If there is any truth to them at all—and I fear there is quite a bit indeed—then perhaps they will prompt an otherwise careless peculiar to take the threat the wights pose more seriously. Even if there is no other good in them, that is enough.

I chose to reprint here one of the most popular wight stories, which is about my own brother. While the writing may be a bit overheated in places, the author thoughtfully consulted with me to get a feel for my brother's proclivities and patterns of speech, and the central action of the story—hunting for peculiars at a local asylum—was for many years a common practice among wights.

WINDOW-SHOPPING AT BEDLAM

A TRUE TALE OF TERROR IN THREE PARTS

BY *FARISH OBWELO*

AUTHOR OF *The Birdmonger of Butcher's Row*

WINDOW-SHOPPING AT BEDLAM

A TRUE TALE OF TERROR IN THREE PARTS

by

FARISH OBWELO,

AUTHOR OF *The Birdmonger of Butcher's Row*

PART I

In a grand town house in the most expensive building in all of London, before a wide window whose high vantage made the pedestrians in Green Park look like toys, there stood a man. He was naked but for a white towel tied round his waist, and in the strong gray light his hairless skin glistened with pear-scented lotion that made him feel tingly and clean. He was slightly fat and bald as a stone and, despite being so old that no one knew quite how old he was, he looked in many respects like a giant baby. He was called Caul, though he'd been known by other names through the years, like Basil and Balthazaar and formerly, as a boy, Jack. Some still called him that, though most called him Caul or Mr. Caul or sometimes Mr. Jack Caul. It was best not to call him anything, though, nor to have any dealings with him at all, if one could help it.

"Ehm. Hallo, sir?" came a voice from behind.

Caul spun around. The new maid was poised tentatively in his office doorway. "Eyes on your shoes," he barked. "I don't like to be looked at."

"I ain't, sir. I just came to say I'm finished. I done the carpets, waxed the floors, and bleached the stairs."

The nearly naked man frowned. "And the windows?"

"With a ten-centimeter cloth, like you said."

He held up his thumb and index finger. "*Tiiiiny* circles?"

"Yessir."

Caul rubbed his chin for a moment, then hit upon something. "What about the walk-in freezer?"

The woman's brow knit together. "You never mentioned . . ."

"It's a room of the house like any other. Just because it's cold, does that mean it's impervious to dirt?" He tapped his bare foot on the spotless floor.

"I—" she began. Then, in a small voice: "Please, sir. I'm due home."

"You will not leave until you have finished your work," he said. "If you're worried about the cold, I'll have Dogsbody fetch you an overcoat."

After she'd gone, Caul removed his towel and threw it in the trash. He never wore anything that touched his bare skin more than once. Just as he never used maids more than once.

He slid on a robe made from lustrous vicuña and pulled the bell for Dogsbody. His flunky took three minutes and a half to appear, which Caul passed in great irritation, flipping through mail-order catalogs for exotic meat that had begun to pile up on his desk. When the man shuffled in, Caul grimaced at the sight of him. His skin was pallid and flaking, his hair a mess, and he was dressed in the clashing styles of several anachronistic eras. He looked as if he'd been put through a laundry mangle.

"You're particularly frightful this morning, Dogsbody. What's the matter with you?"

"I've developed a touch of loop-lag, milord. All this shifting about plays havoc with my constitution, I'm afraid."

"It never used to bother you. Are you getting soft in your second century? Longing for a life of repose?"

"Not at all, milord."

"Perhaps I've been driving you too hard. Once Mortenson has eaten his fill, you may rest a while. Regardless, you're to be properly groomed when you report to me."

"Yes, milord."

Mortenson was Caul's hollowgast, and lately he had developed a ravenous appetite. It had gotten to the point where a meal of normals could no longer sate him, and he moaned perpetually in his basement cage, so loudly neighbors had complained of the noise. Only a peculiar would do, and Caul knew if he was denied the pleasure too long, he might turn against his masters.

"And take off that damned Elizabethan collar, Dogsbody. It gives the impression that you'd rather be somewhen else. You aren't feeling nostalgic, are you?"

"I suppose I prefer the old styles, milord. They remind me of home."

He flung the catalog at Dogsbody and it smacked him in the face. "*Now* is our home! No longer will we allow ourselves to be prisoners of the past!" Caul stood up and began to pace. "Did you pay no attention at all to yesterday's address?"

"I did, milord. I thought it excellent."

"It was," Caul said absently, then waved his hand. "Never mind, there are more pressing matters to deal with than your grasp of current events. Namely: my package. Lord Belphegor said he was sending a crate of salted heads by special courier. Has it arrived?"

"Not yet, milord. Lord Belphegor asked me to remind you that it is coming via submarine, through hostile territory, across three changeovers."

"Yes, yes, Lord Belphegor and his endless logistical excuses." He let out a petulant sigh. "We must get Mortenson something peculiar to eat. *Today*."

"In that case, perhaps you'd care for a little sport, milord."

Caul snapped his fingers. "That's a capital idea, Dogsbody. I haven't been on a hunting expedition of my own in ages. Why let the lords have all the fun?"

"Very good, milord. Where shall we hunt?"

"How about the Ragged School at Spitalfields?"

"Picked clean, I'm afraid, by Lord Holgoth's men, week before last."

"The orphans' home, then."

Dogsbody consulted a small book he kept in his pocket. "Burned down."

Caul harrumphed. "Never mind, I know just the place. Fetch my knife and meet me by the elevators in five minutes. Take off that atrocious collar. And don't forget to kill the maid."

Dogsbody bowed. Caul watched him shuffle out. He didn't generally allow persons of such demonstrable weakness to serve in his Glorious Revolution, but the length of Dogsbody's tenure made him a special case. They'd been through the Black Fire together, and the living Hell of hollowdom (with the pure white eyes to prove it)—side by side since the early days—since before the Great Schism, when there was no such thing as wights or hollowgast. When they were all simply peculiar.

PART II

"Warden. Two gentlemen here to see you."

The lackey stepped aside to allow two men into the warden's office. They had no appointment but were respectably dressed, one in a boater hat and the other in a bowler, and they wore smoked glasses indoors, which the warden thought strange. But strange people were his stock in trade, and on that particular morning he was quite busy, so he didn't bother to mention it.

"Normally, I insist my visitors make an appointment, but I'm told you have some urgent matter to discuss."

"We should like to view your madmen," said the shorter man in the boater hat, his voice high and grating.

"And women," added the taller one. "We don't discriminate."

The warden squinted at the men. An odd combination of smells had wafted in with them, like stewed pears and liniment oil, which reminded him of visits to an old-age home. "Penny-show Tuesdays are a thing of the past," he said. "The ministers thought it cruel, and I can't say I disagree. Only family and persons on official business are allowed in."

"That's fine," said the taller one in the bowler hat. "As it happens, we *are* here on official business."

He drew a coin purse from his coat and dropped it onto the desk. A few coins rolled out. Gold ones. "I hope this will be sufficient," he said with an oleaginous smile.

The warden, who considered himself to be of unimpeachable moral character, and who had never accepted a bribe of any sort (excepting, arguably, the dowry from his son's marriage to that disappointing girl), was about to lose his temper. He was about to tell the men to remove themselves from his office and his asylum at once, lest he call the police. But then the men removed their dark glasses, and he saw that beneath them their eyes were pure white, and as he stared—because he couldn't help but stare—a strange, cold feeling came over him which snuffed out all his aggravation. He glanced quickly toward the door. Seeing that the lackey was gone and they were for the moment unobserved, he opened a drawer in his desk, raked the coins into it, and closed it again.

"Right this way, gentlemen."

PART III

The warden led Caul and Dogsbody down a long hall, past an office where a hunchbacked functionary was scribbling in ledger books, then out into a courtyard garden killed by winter, where a cold breeze made the dead leaves dance. An imposing brick building loomed up ahead. It had been grand once; now its bricks were worn and stained, and through its cracked windows they could hear the voices of the inmates, laughing, braying, shrieking.

They came to a heavy door. The warden opened it, and they entered a small vestibule where they were confronted with two staircases. One went up into the light, the other down into the dark.

"Which would you like to visit?" the warden asked, apparently deaf to the inmates' horrible noises. "The curables or the incurables?"

"Whichever are the most deranged," Caul answered.

"Incurables it shall be."

They started down the dark staircase. At the bottom they arrived at another heavy door, then proceeded down a stone passage suffused with gloom and dampness, its ceiling so low the warden had to remove his hat. Up and down the corridor the men howled in their tiny cells. Some pounded the bars with their heads, the hardest objects they were allowed to keep. Others groaned repetitively or monologued at length in languages of their own invention. Many of the poor souls were manacled to the floor, and the noise of their clanking chains and bestial shouts was enough to drive anyone who wasn't already mad upon entering the building thoroughly so. Caul closed his eyes and held an open hand behind his ear, as if enraptured by a passage of beautiful music. "Lovely, lovely!" he shouted over the din. "Hear that, Dogsbody?"

"What's that, milord?"

"The true voice of man!"

They proceeded down the corridor, Caul stopping before each cell to examine its inhabitant, while the warden recited some horrifying fact about them, hands crossed behind him like a museum docent. "This blackguard believes he's the King of France," he said of a man who'd fashioned a limp crown for himself out of soiled rags.

Inside the next cell, a man was pacing rapidly between the narrow walls. "This one made stew out of his own wife and baby," the warden announced. "Though he had a cupboard packed with food."

"Oh no," said Caul, clicking his tongue disapprovingly. "Never your *own* wife and baby."

The man went on pacing. Snowflakes fluttered into the cell through a tiny barred window that had no glass in it. Caul took note of this. "Won't he freeze to death?" he asked, merely curious.

"Cold's good for 'em," the warden explained. "Keeps their delusions in check. And the stench."

"Yes, it is a bit ripe in here."

"Miasmatic," noted Dogsbody.

They inspected the cells of a dozen more inmates, some positively buzzing with manic energy. Finally, they came to a cell so quiet Caul thought it empty. The warden had to point out the prisoner, crouched silently in a darkened corner.

"Stand up!" barked the warden.

"Come over here so these gentlemen can get a proper look at you."

The figure stood and moved into the weak light. He was a boy of about fifteen, scrawny and small, a mop of wiry red hair atop his head. His eyes were wide and swimming with fear.

"Why, this one's just a lad," said Caul, suddenly curious.

"And madder than any of 'em," the warden warned.

"He doesn't seem so. Look, he's quite calm."

The warden shook his head knowingly. "Thinks he's a *fish*, of all things. Someone caught him about to take a flying leap from the Tower Bridge last week. Said he was going to swim home! He'd be in the morgue now if they hadn't pulled him off the parapet." He laughed. " 'Twas his own auntie who committed him. 'Safest place for him,' she said."

Caul turned to the boy in the cell. "Is that right, my beauty? Are you mad?"

"Yes, sir!" the boy replied confidently. "Quite."

"But isn't that odd! A madperson who knows they are mad."

The boy began to put on a show, hopping about the cell and flapping his arms. *"I'm a fish! I'm a fish!"* he sang. *"I can breathe underwater!"*

"Yes, my dear, I believe you. I'll bet you can."

Something in the way he said it made the boy uncomfortable. He cooled his antics a little, let his arms settle back to his sides.

"I'll bet you can do other things, too," said Caul in a low voice. "Tell me. What else?"

"N-nothing," the boy stammered.

"Now, don't be modest, dear. I know talent when I see it. In fact, I pride myself on my ability to recognize it in people."

"Please, sir, I've no idea what you're—"

"What about your auntie?" He looked disgusted. "What can *she* do?"

The boy's face paled. "Nothing!"

"Nonsense," Caul said. Then, in a vicious whisper: *"I'll bet she can fly."*

The boy took a step backward. "No!"

"What's this about?" said the warden, growing impatient. "Come along, I haven't got all morning."

Caul turned to him. "Warden, you've made a grave mistake. This boy isn't mad at all!"

"I beg your pardon?"

"Yes I am!" insisted the boy.

Caul pressed himself against the bars and stared down the boy while speaking to the warden. "He really is a fish. Not at the moment, of course. But if you threw him into the Thames, I guarantee you he would sprout fins and swim away."

"No, I wouldn't!" cried the boy.

"You really must make up your mind," Dogsbody said to him. "Are you or aren't you?"

The boy fell to his knees, crying. "I'm not, I'm not! I'm not what he says!"

Now Caul got down on his knees, too, shouting through the bars: "Your auntie thought we'd never find you here, did she? Thought you'd blend in!"

"No, no!"

Caul turned to the warden. "This boy is perfectly sane, and I demand you release him into my custody."

"No! Don't let them take me!" cried the boy.

"You're madder than he is!" said the warden.

"Pity," said Caul, getting to his feet. "I was afraid you might say that." Something glinted in his hand. The warden saw it and started to run, but Caul was quicker.

Caul lurched forward and his arm flew out. The warden stumbled and fell, a knife buried in his gut.

The inmates who'd seen it screamed with delight. Caul bent to retrieve the blade from the dying man's body, then walked the length of the corridor with it held out before him, dripping blood. When he reached the end, he turned smartly and took a theatrical bow. The inmates' howls threatened to shake down the walls.

Then a tall, thin man came jogging toward them down the hall, shouting Caul's name. "Your lordship!" It was Ivan Illytch, a wight in his employ. "Mortenson has escaped. He broke out of his cage and is terrorizing the Leadenhall Market."

Caul kicked the ground. "Damn it. He's gone and spoiled his appetite, the glutton."

"Just when we were getting to the fun part," said Dogsbody.

"Isn't that always the way?" said Caul. He turned to the boy in the cell. "I'm afraid you'll have to meet my hollowgast another day. In the meantime, Ivan Illytch will show you to your new home."

The boy had curled himself in a far corner of the cell, as if he could make himself invisible. Which, Caul thought to himself, perhaps he could. In any case, he would know soon enough.

"Please, sir," the boy groveled. "Don't hurt me!"

A toothy smile broke across Caul's face. "*Hurt* you? I wouldn't dream of it, my beauty. I daresay you'll like it where you're going. You'll see. Lots of children your own age to play with. You'll make ever so many friends!"

And then he walked away, leaving the boy in tears and Dogsbody to retrieve the dead warden's keys.

BITS, BOBS,
SUPERFLUOUS
ODDMENTS

Fistibumps are permissible only if a bone-mender is present.

In Séance Chess, one plays against a mentalist channeling the spirit of a long-dead chess master, in this case that of Wilhelm Steinitz, whose skull is propped nearby.

Peculiar Games and Entertainments

We peculiars are as fun-loving as anybody, but because living in loops means that each day is in most essential ways just like the one that came before it, special effort is sometimes required to entertain ourselves. None of the normal diversions of life are available to us: There are no unexpected weather events to keep us on our toes, no circuses or theatrical shows arriving in town that we haven't already attended many times. It's the same with the radio or television, if your loop is fortunate enough to include one; pretty soon everyone can recite each program word for word. (It's just as well. Crowding around a wooden box to watch something in dumbstruck silence, like a lot of hypnotized donkeys, has never been my idea of a good time.)

So we make our own fun. Fortunately, we're quite good at it, and have developed all manner of peculiar entertainments and parlor games to keep ourselves occupied.

Here are a few time-honored favorites that you can try in your own loop. Reproduced in part from *Entertainments for Peculiar Parties* by Millicent Wegg, Esq and *What Shall We Do To-Night?* by Leger D. Mayne.

····➔ HOWL, HOLLOW, HOWL ✦····

A player is selected to be the "ymbryne." He or she is blindfolded, seated on a pillow or large cushion on the floor. The other players are called "hollows" and sit in a circle around the ymbryne. The ymbryne is then spun around two or three times. Taking the pillow, the ymbryne then goes to one of the players and puts it on their lap. The ymbryne sits on the pillow without touching the hollow with their hands (to maintain the anonymity of the hollow). As the ymbryne sits down, squashing the hollow, the ymbryne says, "Howl, hollow, howl!" and the hollow beneath them makes awful howling noises. If the ymbryne identifies the hollow from the squeak, that player becomes the ymbryne; otherwise the ymbryne returns to the center and is spun around again, and the hollows can take the opportunity to swap places.

····➔ JOHNNY'S LOST HIS HEAD ✦····

This game is played by teams of two, plus an audience to judge the winner. One team member plays the "body" and the other the "head." Whichever team stages the most convincing decapitation is declared the winner. *Peculiars who can remove their heads may not play.*

Please don't play this game in public.

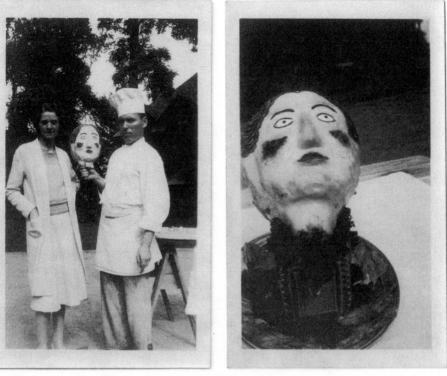

The winner and her delicious prize.

One clever way to "lose one's head" requires a bit of artistry, but the effect is quite chilling and should not be exposed without warning to persons with nervous disorders. A large table draped with cloth that reaches the floor should be placed in the center of the room. A peculiar with long, silky hair should lie on their back under the table, with all of the body hidden but that part of the face above the bridge of the nose. The hair is combed down to look like a beard. A face is painted on the cheeks and forehead, powdered to a deathlike pallor.

The traditional prize awarded after a day of "head games" is a cake baked in the shape of the winner's own head.

Playing a round of "What's in the Hole and Will It Bite?"

Blindfighting is another game that should be played only with a bone-mender in attendance.

····→ LIGHT AS A FEATHER, ←···· STIFF AS A BOARD

One "patient" lies flat on the floor, while ten or twelve "nurses" ring around them, each placing one or two fingers beneath the patient's limbs. The nurses mutter darkly about the patient's condition. "She's looking ill," one will say. "She's getting worse," says another. Finally, "She is dying!" and "She is dead!" Then all participants chant, "Light as a feather, stiff as a board!" while attempting to lift the patient's body using only their fingertips. After several repetitions, a plant among the lifters describes the patient as becoming lighter and lighter, almost weightless. The patient will begin to rise, the effect of which is most unsettling. Of course, *real* levitators shouldn't play, as that will spoil everyone's fun.

····→ SNAIL ORCHESTRA ←····

Did you know? If you place a garden snail upon a pane of glass, in drawing itself along it will frequently produce sounds similar to those of musical cups. To make an orchestra, simply collect as many snails as can be found, and cover a window with them. Better yet, place the snails on crystal glasses with differing levels of water to produce varied tones. The effect can be grating or transcendent, depending on the skill of the snail-wrangler; I once heard Verdi's *Requiem* reproduced note for note by two hundred snails, twelve slugs, and a pair of mating earthworms.

····→ FRIGHTEN THE NORMALS ←····

Once banned, this game is now grudgingly tolerated by ymbrynes as a way for their wards to "blow off steam" and practice manipulating the fragile minds of normals. It should only be played within the confines of a loop containing a population of time-trapped normals. This ensures that their behavior is at least somewhat predictable—the local ymbryne will know which of them are armed and dangerous, for instance, and should be avoided—and more importantly, there is no danger of our secrets being exposed, since the normals' memories are reset each day along with the rest of the loop (at which point you can play another round).

The concept is as straightforward as the name implies: Peculiars compete against one another to see who can give the local normals the biggest scare. Scores are calculated according to their reactions. A shout of "Oh, you frightened me!" is worth one point; a long scream is worth two; screaming and running away, three; screaming and then fainting, four; and anyone who can scare a normal *to death* wins the game automatically. (Points are subtracted if your attempt elicits no reaction. Or worse, laughter.)

As for methods, almost anything is allowed. *No touching* is the only ironclad rule. While it's certainly bound to frighten a normal if you bundle him over your shoulder and toss him off a rooftop, that's simply brutal, and brutality takes no imagination.

One popular scare is to create some kind of monster, either by assembling a costume or distorting one's own features. The Midnight Screecher is a classic example: Made from a shaggy rug and an oven mitt, it's effective, terrifying, and allows for great inventiveness in the noises the "creature" makes.

The Midnight Screecher.

····→ THE "DECEASED DEBUTANTE" ←····

Any peculiar with a bit of either telekinesis or dead-rising talent—or even someone gifted in the art of puppetry—can pull off the deceased debutante. It only requires a skeleton, a flattering outfit, a controller, and someone to be the voice of the cadaverous coquette.

The effect is even more pronounced when the face and hands of the "lady" are hidden behind a veil and gloves, only to be removed at the last moment. I once witnessed Enoch O'Connor pull the deceased-debutante scare on a haughty young gentleman who thought he was God's gift to women. Enoch had been flattering the lad for weeks with faked letters from the father of a supposedly wealthy heiress. When they finally met, Enoch kept the lady's face hidden while seducing him (in a screechy voice) with talk of all the money she was to inherit; only when he agreed to marry her did he pull aside the veil. Enoch won the day when the lad fainted dead away.

····→ THE **NAUGHTY BOY** ←····

Gather an audience, and when they are ready, an accomplice enters the room and tells the "father" of the naughty boy in question that the young man—Tim or Jessup or some name you may invent—is very ill, and the doctor has ordered him to take some medicine and go to bed, but the boy will do neither and is behaving very badly in the next room.

The audience follows the father into the room to see what can be done for such a dreadful child, and they find the boy seated in a high chair, securely tied in. His father takes the medicine in a bowl and a gigantic spoon, and offers it to the boy, who roars, kicks his feet and makes horrible faces. Persuasions, bribes, and threats are tried, until the father, all out of patience, gives the naughty boy a smart rap on the head with the big spoon. With a fearful yell the head falls off behind the chair.

The horrified company, looking behind the chair, will discover the naughty boy was composed of a pillow nicely dressed and fastened to the chair, the feet being the hands of an accomplice thrust into a child's socks and slippers, and the head being the accomplice's, too, so that he can scream, grimace, and even have his head knocked off.

Just before the head falls off.

HOW TO CELEBRATE "LOOP DAY,"
A PRIMER BY HORACE SOMNUSSON

Bother and drat. Loop Day is nearly upon us and I've only just begun to prepare for our celebration! My name is Horace Somnusson, and as usual I'm in charge of decorating; it is widely acknowledged that I'm the only one of Miss Peregrine's wards with any sense of style. Well, I suppose that's not entirely fair—Millard has a *little* style, when he bothers to wear clothes at all—but compared to me his sartorial acumen is like a pebble lost in the shadow of a mountain. I could go on (Bronwyn, shall I compare thee to a brick draped in burlap?). But as I said, I'm short on time and long on festive apparel that needs sewing. And despite my many important responsibilities (and rather against my will), I've been asked by Miss Peregrine to pen a primer on the ins and outs of Loop Day.

Some background for the uninitiated: For many years we lived in a time loop on a small island where every day was just the same as the last. It was a nice-enough day: sunny, a bit balmy, a little rain shower in the late morning. The date was September the third. And because *every* day was that date, and none of us

Myself, dressed in proper Loop Day attire.

in Miss Peregrine's house were born on that date, it was never anyone's birthday. Nor a holiday. If Miss Peregrine had looped Easter, at least we would've been eating chocolate eggs every day. If she had looped the fifth of November, we might've burned Guy Fawkes in effigy and gone bog snorkeling every day. (I wasn't particularly cut up about this, as I don't relish being covered in effigy ash or bog muck.) But September third is not a particularly special day in Britain. So to make up for all the holidays and birthdays we were missing, we celebrated the birthday of our loop, on the one day of the year when the date *outside* the loop matched the date inside it.

How does one celebrate Loop Day? I'll tell you. First, you should really make an effort to dress well for the occasion. (I'm of the mind that you should dress well for *every* occasion, but I will admit some are more befitting of formalwear than others.) Shine your shoes. Iron your shirt. Men: wear a tie. (A clip-on, if you must.) Also, in observance of the rare coincidence of inside- and outside-loop calendar dates, wear a timepiece. On your wrist

Traditional Loop Day fireworks.

will do, but on your clothes or around your neck is preferable. I like to attach a watch to the lapel of my jacket with a safety pin.

Occasionally, the fireworks get out of hand—but no matter, you're in a loop!

As for decorations, I assemble them from all the traditional baubles of holidays we never had the opportunity to celebrate: You may have a Christmas tree, a mask from Carnival or Halloween, a giant wheel of cheese for the Cheese-Rolling Festival, a flute for Worm-Charming Day, or whatever you fancy. The more holiday decorations you can cram in, the better. And no Loop Day would be complete without a gift exchange of some kind. Because we lived on a remote island with no access to shops (or good ones, at any rate), we exchanged things we had either made or found.

Now you're fully prepared to throw an outstanding Loop Day party!

····→ A HANGMAN AND HARRY SHOW ←····

Adapted from the old *Punch and Judy* shows that have been a mainstay in England for centuries, our show features a peculiar named Harry who's always outwitting the normals who want to lock him up, or, more often, put his head in a noose.

All one needs to put on a *Hangman and Harry* show is a puppet stage, some carved wooden characters, and a scene to enact. This one, perennially popular with the girls in my class at the Ymbryne Academy, was nearly banned by Miss Avocet owing to extreme silliness. An expanded and rather more violent version appears in L. D. Mayne's *What Shall We Do To-Night?*

Enoch once staged it with a cast of dead-risen homunculi made from clay, and the effect was quite unsettling.

HANGMAN. Harry, you are my prisoner!

HARRY. What for?

HANGMAN. For having broken the laws of this country.

HARRY. Why, I never touched them.

HANGMAN. And terrified all the women and children.

HARRY. Is that who was screaming?

HANGMAN. Yes, because they saw you kill Mister Bakewell.

HARRY. Mister Bakewell burned my house down and came after me with a bread knife.

HANGMAN. At any rate you are to be hanged.

HARRY. Hanged? Oh dear!

HANGMAN. Yes, and I hope it will be a lesson to you.
    (Erects a gallows on the stage.)

HARRY. Oh, my poor wife and sixteen small children! Most of them twins, and the eldest only three!

HANGMAN. Now, Harry, you are ordered for instant execution. Place your head in the center of this noose.

HARRY. Stop a bit; I haven't made my will.

HANGMAN. A good thought. We can't think of letting a man die until he has made his will.

HARRY. Then I won't make mine at all!

HANGMAN. Quit faffing about and put your head in!

HARRY, *putting his head under the noose.* There?

HANGMAN. Higher.

HARRY, *putting his head over it.* There?

HANGMAN. No, lower.

HARRY. Well, I was never hanged before, so how can you expect me to know where to put my head?

HANGMAN. I suppose I'll have to show you. Now, keep your eye on me. First, I put my head in the noose—just so! *(Puts his head in the noose.)* Then, when I've got *your* head in, I pull the end of the rope.

HARRY, *pulling rope.* Like so?

HANGMAN. Yes, only much tighter.

HARRY. Very good, I think I've got the trick of it now.
(He pulls the rope tightly and hangs the hangman.)

HARRY. Here's a man tumbled into a ditch, and hung himself up to dry! *(The ghost of Mister Bakewell arises and taps Harry on the shoulder.)*

GHOST. I've come back for you.

HARRY. Oh, dear, cannot a peculiar have a moment's peace? What do you want?

GHOST. To carry you off to the land of Abaton, where you will be condemned to the punishment of shaving monkeys!

HARRY. Wait! Who are you after?

GHOST. Why, Harry, the man who was to be hanged!

HARRY. I'm not Harry; there he is! *(Points to hangman.)*

GHOST. Oh! I beg your pardon! Good night! *(Carries off hangman.)*

HARRY, *hitting the sinking ghost.* Good night! Pleasant journey!

> *(Harry sings).*
> *Roo-to-too-it! Served him right,*
> *Now all my foes are put to flight*
> *Ladies and gentlemen all, good night,*
> *To the adventures of Hangman and Harry!*

Useful Phrases in
the Old Peculiar Language

To those who didn't grow up speaking it, Old Peculiar is famously inscrutable. Not only are its rules often contradictory, they change seasonally according to a calendar devised by an ancient peculiar king, Eldric the Indecipherable. The language developed in parallel with all the major Indo-European tongues, closely resembling Saxon at times while incorporating elements of Cornish, Old Norse, Sentinelese, Etruscan, Owlish, the Silbo Gomero whistling tongue, and a smattering of Cro-Magnon grunts that hail from an age before the human larynx had fully descended.

To say that Old Peculiar has a few quirks would be like saying the Tower of London has a few bricks. It has fifty-seven case forms depending on whether a noun is nominative, inessive, comitative, etc., and thus fifty-seven ways of spelling every noun. It has 107 synonyms for "home" but no word meaning "foreign," because when you are perpetually the foreigner, even in lands where you've lived for centuries, the word loses its value.

Old Peculiar boasts the longest word in any language, *lopadotema-choselachogaleokranioleipsanodrimhypotrimmatosilphiokarabomelito-katakechymenokichlepikossyphophattoperisteralektryonoptekephallio-kigklopeleiolagoiosiraiobaphetraganopterygon*, meaning "the feeling of exhaustion one gets after eating too much fish on one's birthday."

Once widely spoken in loops throughout Europe, North Africa, and in Constantinople, our language is still taught at the Ymbryne Academy and used conversationally in scattered outposts among the Hebridean Islands and the Atlas Mountains. Additionally, many of our ancient texts were written in Old Peculiar, and anyone who wants to study them should attempt to master it. While a full knowledge of Old Peculiar is in most cases neither practical nor necessary, it would serve you well to at least memorize a few phrases, if only to impress your friends or charm an old ymbryne the next time you run into one.

I see the worms haven't eaten you yet.

How pleasing that your grave-hole remains empty.

Traditional greetings in Old Peculiar.

···→ A FEW BASIC PHRASES ←···

Hello ☞ *Wyrmæte nu þu biþ.*
LITERAL TRANSLATION: "I see the worms haven't eaten you yet."

Goodbye ☞ *Byþ egle empty þenden þu mæg haelf.*
LITERAL TRANSLATION: "May your grave-hole remain empty until next I see you."

Thank you ☞ *Ic wære feðerhama slite ðe wes.*
LITERAL TRANSLATION: "I would tear off my wings for you."

I'm sorry ☞ *Ic þe slím under þu héla.*
LITERAL TRANSLATION: "I am the mud beneath your feet."

I'm hungry ☞ *Ic cuðe biþ gléd pouppe.*
LITERAL TRANSLATION: "I could eat a burning turd."

···→ OTHER USEFUL PHRASES ←···

This is too many noodles. ☞ *Þes sy offer monegum knudleae.*

Can it be sewn back on? ☞ *Mæg beséowian hu eft oftihð?*

I'm too depressed to go out tonight. ☞ *Ic hreo hyge on feran to niht.*

God, how long is this movie? ☞ *God, hu þenden þes egesan bewlátung?*

This isn't my real face. ☞ *Þes ne sy min soþ andsýn.*

Can you direct me to the catacombs? ☞ *Maeg þu cyð ear byþ neóbedd?*

···→ WORDS WITH NO DIRECT ←···
ENGLISH TRANSLATION

Gorettungæmtianfeornes
The act of gazing vacantly into the distance.

Heáfferblædglíwungblædhyngran
Weeping that turns suddenly to laughter, then snacking.

Becarcianbrūceþbrȳcþgaldorsorgeuncergehierstgeniðle
The anxiety of enjoying a song while worrying that the other people listening
are not enjoying it as much as you are.

AtánonollmúþaungerýdeunderngeweorchwÆte
When the roof of your mouth feels rough after eating certain breakfast cereals.

[Two high-pitched grunts and a long owl hoot]
The burned-toast smell left behind by a collapsed loop.

····➔ COLORFUL SAYINGS ◀····

Nu hit ys on swines dome, cwæð se ceorl sæt on eoferes hricge.
" 'It's up to the pig now,' said the man sitting on the pig's back."

Cræfta gehwilc byþ cealde forgolden.
"Every deceit will be coldly repaid."

Wide ne biþ wel, cwæþ se þe gehyrde on helle hriman.
" 'Things are bad everywhere,' said the woman peering into hell."

Ellen biþ selast þam þe oftost sceal dreogan dryhtenbealu.
"Courage is essential for one who must often suffer great evils."

Wes þu þinum ymbrynum arfæst symle, þa þec geornast to gode trymmen.
"Be respectful to your ymbrynes always, who eagerly urge you to good."

Seoc se biþ þe ferhþgeníðla ieteð.
"The one who eats his enemy's omelette will soon be ill."

Wineleas wonsælig aglæcwíf genimeð hae wulfas to geferan.
"The friendless woman takes wolves as her companions."

Yldo beoð on eorðan æghwæs cræftig.
"Old age has power over everything on earth."

*Ne flit ðu wið ungerád monn. Manegum menn is forgifen ðæt he
spræcan mæg, swiðe feawum þæt he seo gesceadwis.*
"Don't argue with an idiot. Many have the power of speech; very few of wisdom."

Gif ðu hwæt on druncen misdo, ne wit ðu hit ðam grimbera.
"If you do something wrong when drunk, don't blame it on the grimbear."

Monig mon hæfð micel feax on foran heafde, wyrð færlice calu.
"Sometimes a man has plenty of hair on his head, then suddenly goes bald."

Sceal æghwylc syndrigast alætan lændagas.
"Every peculiar will have to relinquish the days loaned to him."

Æghwæt forealdað þæs þe ece ne byð.
"Everything grows old that is not eternal."

Þyrs náhtlíc sceal on fenne gewunian ana innan lande.
"The naughty giant must dwell alone in the bog."

Cwíþinga bið bunyippe tittum: þu næfre unberéafigendlic
"Complaints are like the bunyip's teats: You'll never run out of them."

Hy héafdu bætera þonne óynos. Būtan þrī héafdu bætera þonne hy.
"Two heads are better than one. But three are better than two."

Hopa nae áwringan coney. Ortruwung est spere ne héafdu.
"Hope is an unsqueezed rabbit. Despair is a pike with no head on it."

⟶ PECULIAR IDIOMS ⟵

WHEN YOU ARE STRUCK DUMB BY SOMEONE'S BEAUTY:
Min hycgan cleweða; nearon stánas min ceole.
"My heart is itchy; there are stones in my larynx."

SAID OF A VERY STUBBORN PERSON:
Þu cuðe scearpen brádlástæx hróf to héafod.
"You could sharpen an ax on top of his head."

WHEN SOMETHING ISN'T YOUR RESPONSIBILITY, YOU SAY:
Hringsetl ne; appui ne.
"Not my circus; not my monkeys."

WHEN SOMEONE DOESN'T NOTICE WHAT'S RIGHT IN FRONT OF THEM:
Þu eagum hlides eac sweard.
"Your eyes are covered with ham."

Important Books
by Peculiar Writers

Since time immemorial, peculiars have treasured books and librar-
ies. In medieval times, peculiars who couldn't find a loop to live in
often worked as scribes, finding a life of monastic seclusion surrounded by books preferable to the hurly-burly of daily life among normals. We've written books, too—too many to list here in toto—though I
hope this sampling will give you some idea of the breadth of our output.

⋯→ FOUNDATIONAL TEXTS ←⋯

You'll find these hard to come by and impractical to carry even if you
should find a copy, but as they are the backbone of our literary heritage,
you should be aware of them.

THE *CODEX PECULIARIS*

Written by a peculiar monk from Constantinople named Theodore the
Hermit around AD 850. Legend has it that a powerful nobleman wanted to
wrest the secrets of peculiardom from Theodore, and when he refused, he
was condemned to be walled up alive and starved to death. Bargaining for
his life, Theodore promised to write a book that encapsulated all peculiar
knowledge—and finish it in a single night. It's thought that the *Codex*'s
calligraphy alone would have taken a diligent scribe twenty years to complete, but—in what is still considered a peculiar miracle—he completed

it. When the non-peculiar nobleman read the *Codex*, it caused him
to go mad, climb to the top of his
castle's battlements, and leap to
his death.

The *Codex* is the largest illumi-
nated manuscript in the world. It
measures several feet tall, is made
from the skins of one hundred and
sixty donkeys, and weighs over 200
pounds. It was once thrown from
an upper-story window to save it

Wrestling with the *Codex Peculiaris*.

from a fire, crushing the two people who attempted to catch it. It is considered a precursor to the *Map of Days*, as it contains early information about
faraway loops, lands, and peculiar folk who passed through the great city
where Theodore lived. It also includes stories about the elder peculiars and
the conflicts involving Abaton and the Library of Souls, a treatise on peculiar anatomy and biology, lists of important peculiars and how to contact
them, and advice for living among normals—which also makes it a precursor to the book you're holding now.

THE *MAP* OF *DAYS*

Perhaps the most important book in all peculiardom, the *Map of Days*
is a giant temporal atlas that marks the location of most known loops.[10]
Once a crucial part of every ymbryne's library, many copies were destroyed in an effort to protect their secrets from the wights. Now perhaps
a half dozen remain of varying quality and completeness. The best of
them, which resides in the Peculiar Archives, is massive in size, printed
on vellum, edged with gold, and filled with colorful maps and margina-
lia. Working under the direction of our greatest cartographer, Perplexus
Anomalous, it took a team of artists and bookmakers a lifetime to create.

The *Map of Days* established the cartographical conventions of loop-
mapping: conventional and political borders are marked lightly or not
at all, as they change so frequently and are of little use while traveling

---

10.   Except those loops that have been purposely hidden.

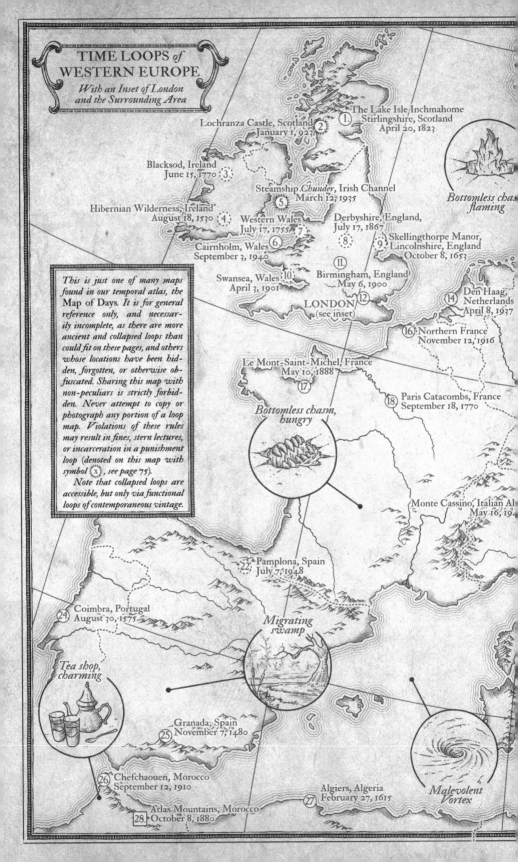

TIME LOOPS of
WESTERN EUROPE
With an Inset of London
and the Surrounding Area

The Lake Isle Inchmahome
Stirlingshire, Scotland
April 20, 1823

Lochranza Castle, Scotland
January 1, 923

Blacksod, Ireland
June 15, 1770

Steamship *Chunder*, Irish Channel
March 12, 1935

Hibernian Wilderness, Ireland
August 18, 1530

Western Wales
July 17, 1755

Derbyshire, England,
July 17, 1867

Skellingthorpe Manor,
Lincolnshire, England
October 8, 1653

Cairnholm, Wales
September 3, 1940

*Bottomless cha
flaming*

Swansea, Wales
April 3, 1901

Birmingham, England
May 6, 1900

Den Haag,
Netherlands
April 8, 1937

LONDON
(see inset)

Northern France
November 12, 1916

Le Mont-Saint-Michel, France
May 10, 1888

Paris Catacombs, France
September 18, 1770

*Bottomless chasm,
hungry*

Monte Cassino, Italian Al
May 16, 194

This is just one of many maps
found in our temporal atlas, the
Map of Days. It is for general
reference only, and necessarily incomplete, as there are more
ancient and collapsed loops than
could fit on these pages, and others
whose locations have been hidden, forgotten, or otherwise ob-
fuscated. Sharing this map with
non-peculiars is strictly forbidden. Never attempt to copy or
photograph any portion of a loop
map. Violations of these rules
may result in fines, stern lectures,
or incarceration in a punishment
loop (denoted on this map with
symbol ⟨x⟩, see page 75).

Note that collapsed loops are
accessible, but only via functional
loops of contemporaneous vintage.

Pamplona, Spain
July 7, 1948

Coimbra, Portugal
August 30, 1575

*Migrating
swamp*

*Tea shop,
charming*

Granada, Spain
November 7, 1480

Chefchaouen, Morocco
September 12, 1910

Algiers, Algeria
February 27, 1615

*Malevolent
Vortex*

Atlas Mountains, Morocco
October 8, 1880

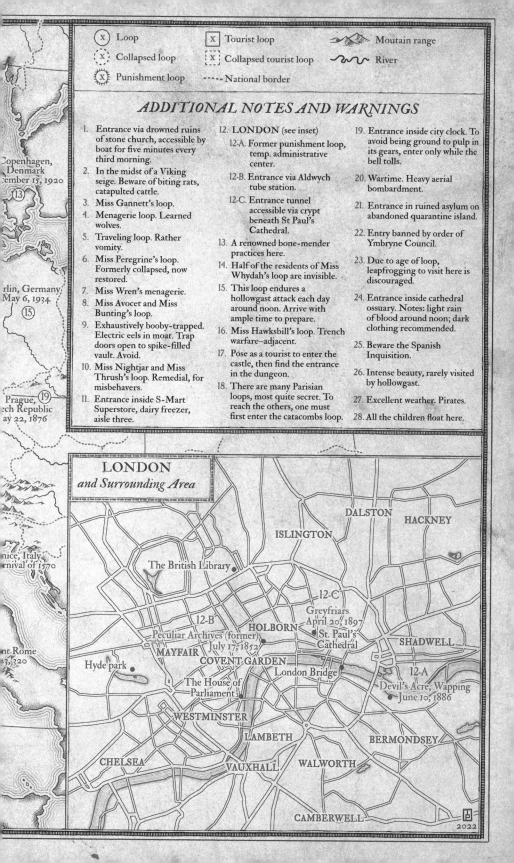

Legend

- Ⓧ Loop
- Ⓧ Collapsed loop (dotted)
- Ⓧ Punishment loop
- [X] Tourist loop
- [X] Collapsed tourist loop (dotted)
- ----- National border
- Mountain range
- River

ADDITIONAL NOTES AND WARNINGS

1. Entrance via drowned ruins of stone church, accessible by boat for five minutes every third morning.

2. In the midst of a Viking siege. Beware of biting rats, catapulted cattle.

3. Miss Gannett's loop.

4. Menagerie loop. Learned wolves.

5. Traveling loop. Rather vomity.

6. Miss Peregrine's loop. Formerly collapsed, now restored.

7. Miss Wren's menagerie.

8. Miss Avocet and Miss Bunting's loop.

9. Exhaustively booby-trapped. Electric eels in moat. Trap doors open to spike-filled vault. Avoid.

10. Miss Nightjar and Miss Thrush's loop. Remedial, for misbehavers.

11. Entrance inside S-Mart Superstore, dairy freezer, aisle three.

12. LONDON (see inset)
    - 12-A. Former punishment loop, temp. administrative center.
    - 12-B. Entrance via Aldwych tube station.
    - 12-C. Entrance tunnel accessible via crypt beneath St Paul's Cathedral.

13. A renowned bone-mender practices here.

14. Half of the residents of Miss Whydah's loop are invisible.

15. This loop endures a hollowgast attack each day around noon. Arrive with ample time to prepare.

16. Miss Hawksbill's loop. Trench warfare–adjacent.

17. Pose as a tourist to enter the castle, then find the entrance in the dungeon.

18. There are many Parisian loops, most quite secret. To reach the others, one must first enter the catacombs loop.

19. Entrance inside city clock. To avoid being ground to pulp in its gears, enter only while the bell tolls.

20. Wartime. Heavy aerial bombardment.

21. Entrance in ruined asylum on abandoned quarantine island.

22. Entry banned by order of Ymbryne Council.

23. Due to age of loop, leapfrogging to visit here is discouraged.

24. Entrance inside cathedral ossuary. Notes: light rain of blood around noon; dark clothing recommended.

25. Beware the Spanish Inquisition.

26. Intense beauty, rarely visited by hollowgast.

27. Excellent weather. Pirates.

28. All the children float here.

LONDON and Surrounding Area

Copenhagen, Denmark
ember 13, 1920 ⑬

rlin, Germany,
May 6, 1934 ⑮

Prague, ⑲
ech Republic
ay 22, 1876

nice, Italy,
rnival of 1570

nt Rome
3, 320

DALSTON
HACKNEY
ISLINGTON
The British Library
12-C
Greyfriars
April 20, 1897
12-B
HOLBORN
Peculiar Archives (former)
July 17, 1852
St. Paul's Cathedral
SHADWELL
MAYFAIR
COVENT GARDEN
Hyde park
London Bridge
12-A
The House of Parliament
Devil's Acre, Wapping
June 10, 1886
WESTMINSTER
LAMBETH
BERMONDSEY
CHELSEA
VAUXHALL
WALWORTH
CAMBERWELL
2022

through the past. It is comprehensive of our current knowledge but by no means complete. There are many loops and regions about which we know little and are mostly blank in our atlases. There is much work yet to be done, and much yet to discover. It's my hope that in the future we will establish relationships with ymbrynes and peculiar cultures worldwide, which will allow us to fill in those blanks and unify our people.

TALES *OF THE* PECULIAR

If you are of the peculiar persuasion (and if you're reading this, I sincerely hope that you are), the *Tales* were likely a formative and beloved part of your upbringing and need little introduction. If, however, you've only just discovered your peculiarity, or grew up in circumstances where no peculiar literature was available, read on.

The *Tales* is a collection of our most beloved folklore. Passed down since time immemorial, each story is part history, part fairy tale, and part

moral lesson aimed at young peculiars. They hail from various parts of the globe, from oral as well as written traditions, and have undergone striking transformations over the years. They have survived so long because they're loved for their merits as stories, but they are more than that, too. They are also the bearers of secret knowledge. Encoded within their pages are the locations of hidden loops, the secret identities of certain important peculiars, and other information that could aid a peculiar's survival in this hostile world.

There are many editions of the *Tales*: exhaustive omnibus editions that span many volumes; portable editions containing only the best-known stories;[11] translations into various languages; editions illustrated with paintings or woodcut engravings. They are best enjoyed read aloud, as per tradition, ideally before a crackling fire on a chilly night, a snoring grimbear at your feet.

---

11. My very own Millard Nullings edited one such edition, a copy of which is proudly displayed in my personal library.

····➔ MODERN WORKS ◈····
OF QUESTIONABLE MERIT

Weight Loss the Peculiar Way
by O. Elephanta

※

I Love You, Virginia Huggins
by V. Huggins

※

The Arrogant Duke's Comeuppance
by T. Leatherback

※

Desperate Longings
by T. Leatherback

※

The Unwelcome Unguent
by T. Leatherback

※

Proceedings of the Second International Committee of Nude Invisibles
by the members of the Second International Committee of Nude Invisibles

※

People Who Don't Know They're Dead, and What to Do About It
by H. Smuggleforth

※

Carrots, and Other Popular Vegetables (self-published)
by H. Somnusson

※

Teaching Your Soup to Talk: A Cookbook
by H. Somnusson

※

Peculiar Planet travel guide
by Various

※

Bombproof Your Chicken Coop: The Husbanding of Explosive Poultry
by B. Wren

⋯⇥ FURTHER READING ⇤⋯

A Farewell to Arms: Hiding Superfluous Limbs in Public (pamphlet)
by D. Blankenforth

✻

A World Lit Only by Fire
by W. Manchester

✻

Curious Creatures in Zoology
by J. Ashton

✻

Embarrassing Moments in Old Peculiar and How to Avoid Them
by E. Avocet

✻

Peculiar Travels on Land and Sea
by Various

✻

Rats, For Those Who Care
by S. Acheron and D. Kelsey-Wood

✻

Strange Cults and Secret Societies (children's edition)
by E. O'Donnell

✻

The Criminal Prosecution and Capital Punishment of Animals
by E. P. Evans

✻

The Inconstant Archipelago: An Atlas of Vanishing Islands
by Nawal Othman

✻

Touring in 1600: A Peculiar Traveler's Complaints
by C. Ogier

✻

Entertainments for Peculiar Parties
by Millicent Wegg, Esq.

Jacob, perhaps one day I will be able to
add your story to this reading list.
If you would ever consider putting pen to paper
and writing it in your own words, I'm certain
you would find many grateful readers.

Parting Thoughts

I realize this must all sound very dire. We are beset on all sides by aggressors, forced to hide in temporal prisons of our own making, threatened with death if we leave our loops for too long or become lost in a present that is now foreign to us. So be it; I do not wish to sugarcoat our situation. Yes, things are grim. But though sometimes it may feel as if all the light has leaked out of the world, as if enemies are ubiquitous and friends very few, take heart: We have survived worse, and we will survive this, too. This war with our former brethren will not last forever. We can and must prevail. Once the last hollowgast is dead and the last wight pacified, there will be much work to do. And you, Dear Reader, will be called upon to pick up a hammer.

A peculiar Renaissance awaits. Until then, take care. Heed the warnings contained herein. Never despair. Above all, know this: Even if this book is as close as you ever come to meeting an ymbryne, and even if you never find a loop or make a peculiar friend, you are not alone.

We are your family.

Tempus edax rerum,
Alma L. Peregrine

INDEX